FRANCESCA

When her sister Francesca disappears, Jamie is determined to unravel the truth. Keeping her identity a secret, she inveigles her way into the household where Francesca lived with her husband, the compelling Alexander Whittaker: wildlife expert, broadcaster — and Francesca's possible murderer. He was seen arguing with her just hours before she vanished, and evidence mounts up that he knew she'd been having an affair. Playing detective becomes a dangerous game for Jamie, especially when she realises she has lost her heart to the prime suspect . . .

SUSAN UDY

FRANCESCA

Complete and Unabridged

LINFORD
Leicester

First published in Great Britain in 1994

First Linford Edition
published 2016

A catalogue record for this book is available
from the British Library.

ISBN 978–1–4448–2733–0

Published by
F. A. Thorpe (Publishing)
Anstey, Leicestershire

Set by Words & Graphics Ltd.
Anstey, Leicestershire
Printed and bound in Great Britain by
T. J. International Ltd., Padstow, Cornwall

This book is printed on acid-free paper

1

Jamie Rivers regarded the man standing in front of her, the man she was currently dating: Rob Gilbraith.

'Are you crazy?' he burst out. 'Do you know that Alexander Whittaker was, and probably still is, the chief suspect for his wife's possible murder? And here you are, intending to go and work for him!'

'That's right, and yes, I do know he was a suspect.'

'You do?' Rob looked surprised.

'Yes. I had a particular interest in following the case.' She paused, unsure whether she should go on or not. 'His wife is my sister,' she finally blurted.

'Your sister?' Rob stared at her, clearly shocked by what she'd just told him.

'Yes.'

'Francesca Whittaker is your sister?'

'Uh-huh.' She nodded.

'But — wasn't her maiden name

Wilde, not Rivers?'

'Yes.' Jamie nodded.

A frown tugged at his brow. 'I don't understand.' He shook his head, his confusion plain to see. 'She lives here, has always lived here — in England — and you've always lived in America. Well, till a couple of months ago.'

'No, I haven't always lived there. For the first three and a half years of my life, I lived here — in England. But when my mother divorced my father and married an American, I moved to the States with her. I subsequently took my step-father's surname, Rivers.'

'Your sister didn't go with you both?'

'No. Francesca was eleven at the time — old enough, my parents thought, for her to decide who she wanted to live with. She chose my father.'

Jamie had often wondered whether her father ever regretted that — regretted splitting his two children up; not reconciling with his wife. Probably not, she'd decided. After all, he'd made no attempt to get Jamie back. And certainly, in her mother's view, he bore the brunt of the responsibility for the break-up. He'd been a workaholic even then, and had continued that way if press reports about him were to be believed. He certainly hadn't made the time to get married again. And, let's face it, you didn't accumulate the sort of fortune he had by slacking. Her mother had told her how lonely she'd eventually felt in her marriage; abandoned, even. So, when Ted came along, the inevitable happened: she fell in love with him.

Curiosity replaced Rob's anger. 'So did you see much of your father?'

'I didn't see him at all. Oh, he sent cards, birthday and Christmas, but even that stopped eventually. I've had no contact with him for twelve, thirteen years. He did send photographs of Francesca, though, from time to time.'

'Did your sister keep in touch?'

'No. My mother tried for a long time, but we never heard from her again.'

Rob's expression softened with pity.

She looked away. The last thing she wanted was pity. She'd long ago accepted her sister's total disinterest in both her and her mother. It didn't hurt anymore; not like it had in her teens, when she'd longed for an older sister to confide in, to share her worries with. In the end, she concluded that Francesca had her life and Jamie had hers, and that was the way it would stay. And the fact was she couldn't have asked for a better father than Ted. He'd treated her as his own daughter — especially when the child he and her mother had longed for failed to materialise.

There had been one photograph in particular she remembered; it had been taken on her sister's wedding day. She'd been standing in a garden, alone, looking very beautiful, very glamorous — and ecstatically happy. Jamie had sent her a card congratulating her. She'd never received any response. Her sister had clearly forgotten she existed — either that, or the address she and her mother had was out of date.

Jamie had managed to keep up with events in her father's life via the American newspapers. He was often featured, being the international businessman he'd become. He'd even been photographed in New York several times. As Jamie and her mother lived in Florida, he'd never bothered to make the journey to visit his youngest daughter. That too had hurt Jamie deeply for a long time, but then she thought — to hell with him. And to hell with Francesca. She'd been with him in New York on one occasion; they'd been photographed together, Francesca hanging on to his arm, clad in what looked like a designer suit, a fur jacket slung over her shoulders. The very epitome of wealth and sophistication.

She smiled grimly then. Francesca — real name Frances. Her mother had told her that at the age of nine her sister had declared that she would only, in future, answer to Francesca. 'It's more mature,' she'd insisted. 'And she's been Francesca ever since,' her mother had said wistfully.

Jamie, despite getting over her hurt at her sister's indifference to them both, had continued to cling to the hope that one day Francesca would get in touch, at least with her mother. She never had — Jamie didn't know why she'd thought she ever would — and now, if the general consensus was right and she was indeed dead, she never would. Just as she would never have the chance to meet up with her father again, for he had died over two years ago; he'd had pancreatic cancer. The report of that came too late, so she was even denied the opportunity to fly to England for his funeral. Once again, there'd been a photograph of Francesca, this time with her husband, Alexander Whittaker. Even that occasion, as sad as it must have been for her, had worked to her advantage. She'd looked hauntingly beautiful in her funereal garb. And that had been the last photograph of her that Jamie had seen. Twelve months later, and almost exactly one year ago, she'd been reported missing. She hadn't been seen since.

Then, as if all that weren't bad enough, four months ago her mother and Ted, her stepfather — he'd legally adopted her when it became clear her father didn't want her back; he'd certainly offered no argument when it had been put to him as a possibility — had been killed in a motor accident. With the disappearance of everyone she cared about from her life, Jamie had decided to return to the land of her birth. And so here she was; and, despite the cruel manner in which her sister had ignored her for the past twenty-one years, she was determined — no, driven — to discover what had happened to Francesca, and if she was still alive to somehow find her.

She'd met Rob soon after she'd arrived two months ago, and since then they'd been meeting a couple of times a week. Hence his interest now, and obvious hurt that she hadn't confided in him earlier.

He was still watching her. 'How did

you find out about your sister's disappearance?'

'Alexander Whittaker is well-known enough in the States for his wife's disappearance and his subsequent arrest to have been splashed all over our newspapers as well as yours.'

'So if you know the whole story, why are you even considering haring off to Devon; considering staying at his house? When he could very well be a murderer?'

'Nothing could be proved against him, that's why he was released so quickly. The police haven't even been able to confirm Francesca's dead — not without a body. She could simply have left him.'

'That's rubbish. You know it; the police know it. What about the earring found by a moorland pool? Cromer Pool, wasn't it? Almost the last place she was seen, incidentally, and with Alexander Whittaker, no less. He's confirmed it's hers. No, I'm sorry, Jamie, she's dead and everything points to him being the killer.'

'The witness only had a view of his back, and Alexander categorically denied having been on the moor that day.'

'And you believe him?' Rob scoffed. 'What would you expect him to do, hold up his hands and say 'Oh, yes officer, I did it — arrest me'?'

'No, because I don't think he did do it, and the police must have believed him as well, otherwise why release him?'

'For goodness sake, he had a clear motive. Surely you'll admit that? Your sister was an extremely wealthy woman. She inherited everything your father had made over the years. In the event of her death, Whittaker would get it all.'

'So in that case, why didn't he leave her body where it would be found? Without proof of death, surely he wouldn't have inherited anything?'

Rob shrugged. 'I don't know what happens in those circumstances.'

And that had been something else that had hurt Jamie at the time of her father's death. He hadn't cared enough about her to leave her anything. She hadn't wanted his money; Francesca was quite welcome to that. No, what had hurt almost unbearably was the fact that as far as she knew, she hadn't even been mentioned in his will. Hadn't been left as much as a memento of him.

'But the truth is there aren't many people who'd turn their noses up at the chance of a fortune like that,' Rob went on. 'Not even Alexander Whittaker. And if she is dead, it will all eventually come to him.'

'Alexander Whittaker must have more money than he knows what to do with. Why would he murder to get more? No, sorry, it doesn't make sense; none of it does.'

'Maybe he isn't as rich as he's cracked up to be. His expenses on those wildlife trips of his must be pretty hefty.'

'I would imagine the television company must reimburse him for those,' Jamie quietly insisted. 'It's no good you trying to persuade me otherwise, Rob. I'm going. He has a deadline to meet and urgently needs an artist to illustrate his latest book. And, hey, I'm an artist. Besides, I need the money he'll pay me.'

'Didn't your mother and step-father leave you anything?'

'Some. Ted was in quite a lot of debt, mainly to the bank it turned out. So they'll be taking most of it.'

'Oh, Jamie.' He regarded her with compassion again.

'Don't worry about me.' She didn't want anyone's pity. 'I can look after myself, but I do need some sort of job.'

'Okay, I can understand that, but why do you have to stay at his house? In Devon of all places?'

'Dartmoor, to be specific. Alexander Whittaker likes the artist he uses to be under his direct control.'

'So as well as being a suspected murderer, he's also a control freak.' He regarded her quizzically. 'Are you going to tell him that you're Francesca's sister?'

'No. I want to do a bit of investigating first.'

'Investigating? Investigating what?'

'Francesca's disappearance, of course.'

'Let me get this straight — you're planning on staying there incognito?' She nodded. 'You actually think you'll succeed in finding out what happened to her when the police, with all their resources, failed?' She shrugged. He snorted. 'You'll never get away with it. Supposing Francesca told him about you?'

'I'll face that if and when it happens. With my change of surname, there's no reason for him to know who I am. He won't have seen a photograph of me because my mother never sent one to Francesca. And I very much doubt that she would have kept one of me, given her complete lack of interest.'

'I could kill that Adrian Bryant,' Rob suddenly burst out.

'Adrian got me this job because I asked him to. Alexander has been unexpectedly let down by his usual illustrator and I asked him, as Alexander's publisher, to recommend me. It's a perfect opportunity for me. He'll think I'm simply an illustrator, nothing more. He'll never suspect my real motive for being there. It could have taken me months to meet him under any other circumstances, and I certainly wouldn't have had access to his home. But apart from that, think what it will do for my reputation. He's a very prestigious author as well as a television personality. His wildlife programmes are watched by millions worldwide.'

'Well, on your head be it.' He paused. 'Does Adrian know Francesca was — is — your sister?'

'No. I simply said that my American agent had mentioned his name as a possible source of work, which is perfectly true. There was no real reason for him to recommend me to Alexander — other than that of desperation.' Jamie smiled fleetingly. 'But now that he has, I don't intend to refuse the opportunity.'

'Well, at least the man recognises talent when he sees it. Presumably Whittaker knows you're American?

'I would imagine Adrian will have mentioned it.'

Bowing to what must seem like inevitable defeat, Rob changed tactics. 'Just promise you'll keep in touch while you're there. How long do you think the job will last?'

She shrugged. 'A month or so, providing I can meet his deadline.'

'When do you go?'

'Tomorrow.'

'Tomorrow!' His dismay was only too evident. 'Well, okay, but ring me when you get there.'

Jamie regarded him warily. He was starting to exhibit signs of an unwelcome possessiveness, and that was the last thing she wanted. She liked Rob well enough, but that was all she felt: liking. They'd only known each other a few weeks, after all. Maybe her stay in Devon would be the perfect time to put some distance, emotionally as well as in miles, between them. For the fact was, she had no intention of forming any sort of long-term relationship, not at this stage in her life, and certainly not with someone she'd only just met.

'I'll try,' she said with deliberate coolness. She may as well start as she meant to go on. 'But I'm going to be rather busy, I would imagine.'

Rob clearly didn't recognise her attempt to cool things, because he went on, 'Right, well, if there's any sign of trouble, ring me, and I'll come down personally and fetch you.'

She sighed. 'There'll be no need for that. I've got my own transport. Remember?' She'd splashed out a couple of days ago and hired a small car for a month, which was one of the reasons she needed a job and quickly. Without an income, and at the rate she was spending, her money wasn't going to last long. Which meant that the sum that Alexander Whittaker would be paying her was simply too good to turn down, whatever Rob thought. But what made it totally irresistible was the fact that she would be staying in Alexander Whittaker's house. Her day-to-day living costs would disappear; at least, she hoped they would. It also meant she could give up her bedsit — for the time being, at any rate, thereby saving even more of her money. If Alexander Whittaker agreed to take her on, and although there was a strict deadline for providing the artwork for his latest book, she'd be in Devon for a month, at least. Which gave her plenty of time to try and solve the mystery of her sister's disappearance. At least, that was what she hoped.

'Well, I wouldn't trust the blighter as far as I could throw him, and neither should you. The first hint of trouble, you leave.'

★　★　★

'You're a woman, and an American to boot.' Alexander Whittaker scowled at Jamie as she stood on the top step of the front entrance to the hugely imposing house that was Moorlands, the house in which her sister had spent her last few years. Although the word 'house' was something of an understatement.

'Mansion' would be more appropriate.

'Oh, dear. Was it my accent that gave me away?' she ironically retaliated. 'Tell me, do you have something against Americans? Or is it just me in particular?'

So Adrian hadn't mentioned her nationality, and it sounded — and looked — as if that would be another black mark against her, making it two if she added that to the fact that she was female; three if she included her readiness to stand her ground and answer back. With three strikes in total, she was well and truly out. She may as well turn round and leave right now. But something way down inside her refused to concede defeat, and so she stood her ground, her demeanour one of defiance.

'I have absolutely nothing against Americans in general,' he bit back. 'The fact is I don't usually commission women.'

'Aah, well there's always a first time.' She decided not to mention that such unabashed sexism must surely be illegal. There was nothing to be achieved in irritating him even more than he already was.

'But it won't be the first time; it will, in fact, be the third. And, I'm sorry to say, I have no intention of repeating those experiences. The wretched women proved totally unreliable, completely missing their deadlines.'

'Surely not as unreliable as the last artist you were employing — if I've understood matters correctly? David Banion, I believe that was? Didn't he up and actually leave rather . . . suddenly?' Jamie smiled then; a smile that, if he'd bothered to look at her properly, he would have seen didn't reach her eyes.

'There were exceptional circumstances for that,' he said stiffly.

'I'm sure there were. After all, he was a man, wasn't he? And a man wouldn't do anything as unprofessional as needlessly running out on you — not like a woman might.' She caught her bottom lip between her front teeth. She could

18

have phrased that last remark a little better, given the circumstances of his wife's disappearance. Her impetuous words could prove to be all he needed to send her packing right now, before she'd as much as set foot over the doorstep. Dear God, why did she never think before she opened her mouth?

But she was saved from such an immediate and humiliating dismissal, because his sole response was a muttered, 'Are all American women this outspoken?'

'I wouldn't know. I can only speak for myself.'

'And you're certainly doing that,' he growled. 'You'd better come in,' he grudgingly invited, immediately turning his back on her to stride through an open door on the far side of the hallway.

'Thank you, I will,' she murmured with more than a touch of exasperation. Really, the man was little more than a graceless boor. Whatever had Francesca seen in him? With her looks, she could have had any man she wanted, surely?

She followed him into a spacious sitting room to find him already standing in front of a marble fireplace, legs planted well apart and arms crossed over his chest. His expression was one of brooding impatience. What was his problem? Anyone would think she'd taken her time in following him. Maybe Rob was right and she shouldn't have come here. Because the possibility that he had killed Francesca was starting to look like a very real one. He certainly looked as if he'd happily throttle her.

She took a moment to look away from him and glance around the room. It was beautifully decorated in shades of apple-green, lemon and ivory; it also had two floor-length windows through which the late August sunshine was pouring. Chairs and settees, deeply cushioned and upholstered in fabric the colour of clotted cream, were interspersed with what looked like extremely valuable antique furniture. Paintings decorated the walls, mainly watercolours; a few of them looked as if they could have been illustrations taken from his books. However the largest one, above the fireplace, was a simply framed oil painting of his wife. Jamie couldn't drag her gaze away from it. It was as if her sister were staring straight at her, a small smile lifting her full lips.

'Funny sort of name for a woman — Jamie,' he unexpectedly declared. 'It's also very misleading.'

'Misleading?'

Although she was pretending not to understand, she most certainly did. After all, Adrian had left her in no doubt that Alexander Whittaker only ever commissioned men; and the name Jamie, a commonly used adaptation of James, bestowed the distinct impression that the artist was a man. 'He'll never agree to a woman,' he'd told her. 'He simply won't employ one.'

'That's sexual discrimination, Adrian,' she'd succinctly pointed out. 'There's a law against that, isn't there?'

Adrian had shrugged. 'Well, he doesn't actually say that, naturally. He just finds some perfectly acceptable reason to turn them down.'

She'd slanted a glance at him. 'With a name like mine, and if you don't tell him, there's a very good chance he won't realise I'm a woman till I get there. By which time, it'll be a bit late for him to say no. And didn't you say he's desperate for someone?'

'We-ell, yes, I did, but he's going to have my guts for garters if I send you. He knows that I'm perfectly well aware of his preference for male artists. In which case, how do I explain sending you?'

'I guarantee he'll agree to me staying.'

Brave words, she'd reflected. The truth was, it was little more than bluff on her part. But she'd needed Adrian to have the necessary courage to let her go to Devon, as well as confidence in her ability to persuade Alexander Whittaker to let her stay once she got there, otherwise her journey to England would have been in vain. Without direct access to Francesca's husband and home, she'd have very little chance of discovering what had happened to her sister.

She swallowed now, mutely praying that she hadn't landed Adrian in too much trouble. Looking at Alexander, however, she wasn't at all optimistic about that, because his steely gaze conveyed the distinct impression that he would be more than capable of despatching her back the way she'd come, sexual discrimination laws or not. And more than capable of ending Adrian's tenure as his book publisher into the bargain.

'I'm sure you know precisely what I mean, Ms Rivers. Adrian Bryant knows full well that I prefer to commission men for my artwork. Women's paintings are invariably too . . . well, romantic for my taste. But apart from that, as an American, I don't expect you will be familiar with British wildlife.' He frowned. 'I can't think what possessed him.'

'Could it be the fact that he couldn't find another artist willing to down tools and come straight away?' Jamie's tone was a sharp one, as exasperation with this arrogant man finally overwhelmed her.

'And you were prepared to 'down tools and come straight away'?' His tone was a sarcastic imitation of her own. 'Why? No other work?'

The question was a provocative one calculated, she suspected, to make her lose her temper and say something rash — even more rash than she'd already been, thereby giving him a valid excuse to tell her to go. Well, she wasn't going to give him the opportunity. She'd keep her cool, no matter how great the provocation.

'Or maybe you and Adrian colluded in the deception?'

'We certainly did not.' Which was perfectly correct. Adrian had only very reluctantly agreed and, in her opinion that didn't make it collusion. Still, she wasn't about to admit to it being her idea to be economical with the truth, not unless she was absolutely compelled to. Because he'd be bound to tell her to leave if she did, and she'd do anything to avoid that; anything at all. If she didn't get to stay here at Moorlands, she'd have no earthly chance of discovering what had happened to her sister.

His eyes narrowed at her. 'I presume you have all the necessary papers to permit you to work in England? I don't want to be accused of employing an illegal immigrant in the unlikely event of you remaining here.'

'You won't be.' He didn't need to know that she was British by birth.

'So . . . ' His gaze travelled all over her at that point. 'What are we to do now, Ms Rivers?'

'Maybe dispense with the formalities? I'd much prefer it if you called me Jamie.'

He inclined his head. 'Certainly, if

you wish it. You may call me Alexander — or, as most people do, Xander for short.'

Jamie was forced to hide her smile at that point. His haughty manner was more appropriate for the nineteenth century, rather than the twenty-first.

'Which part of America do you come from?' he asked.

'Florida.'

'You're a long way from home. How do your family feel about you being here?'

'My family are all dead. That's why I've come. I decided I need a fresh start.'

She found herself on the verge of telling him that she had lived in England until she was three, but then decided that might not be altogether wise. He might ask even more questions, such as who her family were. No, the most sensible thing would be to keep that to herself, at least for the time being.

For a split second she thought she

glimpsed compassion within his eyes as he murmured, 'I'm very sorry to hear about your family.' And just as she had with Rob, she found she didn't want his compassion; she wanted the truth. The truth of what had happened to her sister. But his sympathy swiftly evaporated and, in both manner and expression, he reverted to what she presumed was a normal emotion for him: cool indifference.

'Where are you staying now?' he went on to ask.

'I'm renting a bedsit just outside of Reading.'

He glanced at his watch and said, 'In that case, as it's almost six thirty, you'd better stay the night and we'll discuss our options tomorrow. You'll join us for dinner, of course?'

It was at that juncture that Jamie's stomach gave a loud grumble.

'Which I'd guess from the sounds coming from the region of your stomach you're more than ready for.' His mouth twitched as he spoke and, for the first time, Jamie glimpsed amusement within his gaze.

Her heart accordingly gave an energetic flip. He might be the most arrogant and rude man she'd ever had the misfortune to meet, but he was also undeniably the most handsome.

'We eat at eight o'clock generally,' he went on. 'I'm sure tonight will be no exception.' He walked to the door and pressed a button on the wall.

The subsequent pause in hostilities gave Jamie the chance to study him. She had of course seen him on television several times — his programme was regularly screened in the US — but those viewings had in no way prepared her for the sheer impact of him in the flesh. He was tall — six foot one or two, she guessed; and looking at his powerful build, it was evident that he worked out on a regular basis. Huh! He probably had his own private gym somewhere here in this palatial house. His hair was the colour of malt whisky; his eyes, she had already noticed, were an unusually light brown, almost amber. As he swung back to her, she saw that his nose was very slightly aquiline and his jaw line looked as if it was fashioned from steel, and his mouth was chiselled. Yet for all that, the full bottom lip hinted at a certain sensuality. Just for a second, she wondered what it would feel like to have that mouth pressed against her own.

Belatedly, she realised that he was also staring at her, clearly taking note of her intent appraisal. Several minute gold flecks appeared within his eyes and he seemed about to say something. However, before he could do so, the door opened into the sitting room and a small plump woman walked in. She'd obviously been summoned by the pushing of the bell. Good grief, the place was like a stately home.

'Yes, Mr Xander?'

Yes, Jamie mused, definitely a stately home with the residents — this woman included — still residing in the nineteenth century.

'Ah, Mrs Skinner. Would you show Ms Rivers to the room that David was using? She'll be staying the night, at least.'

Jamie saw the woman's glance dart from Alexander to herself. She made no effort to hide her surprise. All she said, however, was, 'Certainly. Would you come this way, please?'

Jamie looked back at her host once more. When he didn't speak, she said, 'Eight o'clock then?'

He nodded. 'You'll be meeting my brother at dinner, so don't worry, you won't have to deal with me on your own.' He gave a grim smile. 'I'm sure you'll find a champion in Brad. He's very partial to a lovely woman.'

Jamie caught the briefest flash of bitterness in the amber eyes, right before she turned and followed the small woman from the room.

'Do you have any luggage, Ms Rivers?'

'Yes, I'll go get it. It's in the car.'

'Don't you worry. My Dennis will get it for you. Is the car locked?'

'No. It's very kind of you, Mrs Skinner.' As it was the first kindness she had met with since arriving at Moorlands, it brought the sting of tears to Jamie's eyes. She put her uncharacteristic weepiness down to her fatigue in the aftermath of the long and fairly difficult journey here and then the unwelcoming and critical reception she'd received upon arrival.

It was no comfort to reflect that she'd brought it upon herself entirely. Adrian had warned her, but in her usual headstrong fashion she'd ignored his advice, his and Rob's.

'My Dennis,' the woman she presumed was Alexander Whittaker's housekeeper said, 'acts as gardener-cum-handyman-cum-chauffeur when needed, and I'm the housekeeper in case you're wondering.'

Mrs Skinner led her up a sweeping flight of stairs to a large galleried landing. 'I presume you're here about doing the artwork for Mr Xander? We were all expecting a man.' She flicked a kindly smile over her shoulder at Jamie.

'So I gather,' Jamie drily remarked.

'Given you a hard time, has he?'

'You could say that.'

'Oh, he'll come round, I'm sure. You don't want to take too much notice of him. His bark is a great deal worse than his bite, you can rest assured of that.'

Jamie fervently wished she could believe that.

2

A long, hot bath did much to restore Jamie's spirits, as well as her sense of proportion. Alexander Whittaker was just a man, after all, not the devil himself. So he'd sent her away again — so what? She'd find a job, even if it was just waiting on tables somewhere. She'd done it before; she could do it again. And somehow — she wasn't sure how at the moment, if she wasn't permitted to stay here at Moorlands — she'd do what she came here to do: find her sister.

In a calculated gesture of defiance, and also of pride in the fact that she was indeed a woman, she selected one of her most feminine dresses to wear. It was fashioned out of a deep blue crepe de Chine and it unashamedly clung, outlining the curves of her breasts and hips. There was no mistaking her for anything other than a woman. It was a marked contrast to how she'd looked on arrival, dressed as she'd been in a loose-fitting shirt and a pair of old but comfortable pair of jeans.

She wondered what Alexander Whittaker would make of it. She still thought of him by his full name; somehow Xander seemed too familiar for someone who'd only just met him. And he definitely looked more like an Alexander. However, as she was almost certainly going to be given her marching orders the next day, it didn't really matter. In fact, now that she considered things, her gesture was an empty one. It didn't matter how attractive she made herself look, she was still a woman; and as he had made more than clear, he refused to employ a woman.

She pulled a face at her reflection. So much for her going against Rob's wishes — which reminded her, she'd better call him before he called her.

'Everything okay?' was his first predictable question. 'I've been worried.'

'Everything's fine.' She paused before saying, 'Other than the fact that I'm a woman.' She hadn't told him about Alexander's aversion to women artists, so he was understandably surprised.

'What on earth do you mean?'

'Alexander Whittaker insists on his artists being men.'

'Did you know that before you left to go there?'

'Yeah.'

'And you still went?'

'Yeah.'

'Presumably you were gambling on the fact that from your name he'd assume you were a man and so would agree to see you?'

'Yeah.'

'And now he knows you're not?'

'I leave again in the morning. He did have the grace to invite me to stay overnight, though,' Jamie drily retorted.

'I have to admit it's something of a relief to hear that you'll be returning almost straightaway.'

'Well, don't let the relief go to your

head, because I have every intention of trying to persuade him to let me stay. I can't see he's got much choice, so it's worth a go. He won't get another artist on such short notice.'

Total silence met this statement; but then, to her surprise, he said, 'Well, as I said before — be it on your own head.'

'It will be. Night, Rob. I'll be in touch.'

As Jamie walked back to the full-length mirror, her expression was a reflective one. She eyed herself in the glass, her determination to emphasise her femininity ebbing away. Was she making a terrible mistake? Would the clingy dress and four-inch heels simply make Alexander even more conscious of the fact that she wasn't a man; make him even more determined to tell her to leave? Maybe she ought to change. Something more business-like? Trousers, maybe? Sensible shoes? However, as the only sensible shoes she'd brought with her were trainers, that option was out of the question. She sighed. She'd given in to impulse — something she did far too often. It had landed her in trouble more times than she cared to think about.

She tilted her head to one side, considering her reflection. She'd always deemed herself lacking in the ingredients for true beauty. Her violet-blue eyes were her best feature, along with their long, dark, curling lashes. Her nose was straight, slightly too long for her taste; her mouth — well, she supposed that wasn't too bad: full-lipped, naturally rose-pink. She'd accentuated this with her favourite lipstick. She also possessed high cheekbones and a neatly rounded chin. But undermining all of that was her height — or lack of it, rather; she was too short at 5 feet 4 inches and, in her opinion, such an obvious lack of stature made her look plump, given her 38-26-37 figure. Which was why she'd opted for high heels. They gave her a bit more . . . well, presence. And they did enhance the curves of her legs. Since her teens she'd longed to be at least 5 foot 7 or even 8 inches, with neater breasts, sleeker hips, and longer legs. More like Francesca, who'd inherited her father's genes, while Jamie had got her mother's.

Oh well, Alexander would have to take her as she was. Or not. She glanced at her wristwatch. It was too late to change into something else anyway; it was three minutes short of eight o'clock. And she still had to find her way back to the sitting room — or should it be the dining room? And where the hell was that anyway?

She ran a hand over her honey-blonde hair. That was another thing; she invariably had trouble controlling the shoulder-length, maddeningly way-ward locks. No matter what she did — left them down, put them up, applied shedloads of lacquer — they invariably went their own way, and chaos reigned. This evening, in an effort to look at least semi-professional, she'd heaped it all onto the top of her head, hoping it would stay there. But as she

rushed from the bedroom towards
where she hoped she'd find the landing
and stairs down, she felt several strands
work loose to curl down over her ears.
She debated returning to her room to
put things right, but then decided, as
she wasn't sure she remembered the
way, so vast was the house, she hadn't
got the time. All she could do was hope
the casual style would look intentional.
For Alexander Whittaker had looked
just the sort who would be a stickler for
punctuality, and she didn't want her
late arrival to add another nail to her
already firmly fastened coffin.

★   ★   ★

Two men awaited her in the sitting
room: Alexander was one, so the other
must be his brother, Brad. She glanced
at the ornate clock on the mantelpiece
— it read two minutes past eight — and
then looked back at the men.

'Sorry I'm a bit late.' She smiled at
Brad.

39

He looked younger than Alexander, but there was no mistaking they were brothers. He was fractionally shorter and his build was also a tad lighter than Alexander's, but other than his hair being mid-blond rather than whisky-coloured, there wasn't much to choose between them. His ready smile, though, was very different to his older brother's expression. That could indicate anything: disapproval; censure; condemnation, even. Although, for all his inscrutability, his gaze did rake her from head to foot and then back again. Even so, his thoughts remained irritatingly unfathomable. So much so, that she couldn't decide if the dress was a mistake or not; whether it had strengthened his intention to send her packing the next day, or shifted his decision in her favour.

The sight of Brad holding out a welcoming hand, however, was a heartening one. At least someone in this intimidating household looked to be on her side.

He confirmed this impression by saying, 'Welcome to Moorlands, Jamie.

I'm glad you haven't allowed my ogre of a brother to send you packing straight away. I'm Brad, hopeless wastrel and notorious good-for-nothing.' He grinned at her and Jamie found herself smiling back. The younger man's amiability was infectious. It was a pity the infection didn't extend itself to his brother, who was by this time glowering at both of them.

Completely oblivious to the sudden drop in the room temperature, Brad took her by the arm and led her to a table in the window upon which a tray sat, loaded with bottles and glasses. 'Now, what will you have? Perhaps you'd like to join me in a glass of bubbly, by way of a small celebration?'

'Celebration?' She stared back at him. Had she inadvertently interrupted a private occasion?

'Yes. Of the fact that you're here. That's definitely an event worthy of celebration. So, in the absence of a ten gun salute, we'll make do with Champagne. The truth is, it's been a while since we've had a beautiful woman in the house — not since Francesca.' He cast a sideways and noticeably wary glance at Alexander, as if expecting some sort of reprimand.

As it turned out, there wasn't even the mildest of reprimands, but the atmosphere in the room cooled yet again in the wake of his words; it was so cool, in fact, that Jamie felt as if she were standing in a bath of ice.

'That would be lovely,' Jamie hastened to say. 'I love Champagne. Can't get enough of it.'

'What Brad is loath to say is not since my wife Francesca was here,' Alexander put in. 'Haven't you forgotten someone, Brad? Rosamund? She seems to be a fairly frequent visitor these days.'

Brad handed Jamie some Champagne. 'Ah, but it's not me she comes to see, is it? And, in any case, she doesn't compare to this fair damsel.'

Jamie all but choked into her glass, prompting a bevy of bubbles to fizz energetically up her nose. She couldn't help herself; she sneezed — as discreetly as she could and into her cupped hand, but even so, both men stared at her, Brad with a grin, Alexander with what looked like tight-lipped derision. But really — fair damsel, for heaven's sake? What age were these two living in? Never mind the nineteenth century. It was more like the middle ages.

And, as if he were determined to aggravate the already strained circumstances, Brad ploughed on, seemingly oblivious yet again to Alexander's deepening frown.

'To compare Rosamund to Jamie is like comparing a glacier to a flame, and I know which one I prefer.' Brad's look fairly smouldered at Jamie.

She felt the beginnings of a giggle in her throat — at almost the same instant that her stomach emitted a loud grumble. Oh God! How much worse could things get?

She swiftly found out. Without as much as a glimmer of humour,

Alexander said, 'I think you'd better hold back on more Champagne, Brad, and push the button for Mrs Skinner to start serving dinner. If we don't get some food into Jamie, I think she might expire before our very eyes.'

★ ★ ★

Not surprisingly, after the unnerving start dinner proved a tense affair, with Brad drinking the best part of a bottle of red wine on his own. 'Of course,' he said at one point, 'all of this — ' He flung an arm wide, indicating the house at large, Jamie could only presume. ' — belongs to Xander. Did you know that, Jamie?'

'Um — no, I didn't,' Jamie managed to stammer. She was feeling more and more uncomfortable. 'But then, I don't think it's any of my business.' It was a mild rebuke, but a rebuke nonetheless.

Brad disregarded it. 'Our dear father believed in the time-honoured tradition of leaving everything to the older son

44

— primogeniture, Jamie. Yes, I know — '
He waved a hand at her, the one that was still holding his knife. ' — like me, you believed that custom to have died out long ago. Not so . . . '

Alexander's harsh tones interrupted. 'I don't think Jamie wants to hear any of this.'

'Oh, really?' Brad sneered. 'Or is it that you don't want her to hear it? You see, Jamie,' he went on as he took another large swig of his wine, 'our father made himself a fortune over thirty years of investing in all the right things and didn't want it divided up. He left the whole damned caboodle — ' He carelessly waved his glass around, managing in the process to slop most of what it contained over his hand. ' — the house, the business, the flat in London, the condo in Florida, the villa in France, and every last bloody penny of his money to Xander. I got nothing; zilch.'

'Brad,' Alexander bit out in vain, because now that Brad had got started he couldn't seem to stop.

'I have to beg for everything I receive. Charming, isn't it? I'm forced to live on handouts. No wonder Francesca turned to — '

'Brad!' Alexander snapped. He had clearly reached the end of his patience. 'That is enough. We don't air family grievances in public.' His features had hardened until they resembled chiselled granite.

'No, we don't, do we?' Brad stumbled to his feet, slamming his glass down, snapping its fragile stem as he did so, and spilling the remainder of the contents over the polished surface of the mahogany table. 'Not the done thing, is it, brother dear?' he sneered. 'After all, people might realise you're not the great chap you're made out to be. Your doting public might get to hear of it, for one thing; and that would never do, would it?'

Jamie looked from one brother to the other in some dismay. 'Um, perhaps,' she said as she, too, scrambled to her feet, 'it might be better if I left you?'

'No, sit down, Jamie,' Alexander curtly commanded. 'Brad will be the one to leave.'

'Oh, don't worry, I'm going.' He gave a snappy bow to Jamie. 'My apologies. You'll have to forgive me. I've had rather a trying day.'

'Come and see me in the morning, Brad,' Alexander again commanded, more gently this time. 'We'll talk then.'

Brad smartly clicked his heels together and mockingly saluted his brother. Jamie quickly hid her smile.

'Yes, brother; anything you say, brother.'

With Brad gone, an uneasy silence descended upon the two people left behind. For the second time, Jamie made to go as well. Alexander's words stopped her. 'I'm sorry about all of that.'

Jamie swivelled her head to look at him. 'Maybe he has a point? It must be humiliating for him to be forced to rely on you for handouts.'

Alexander's brow lowered. 'As you know nothing about it,' he said in a harsh voice, 'I would appreciate you

47

keeping your opinions to yourself.'

She took a deep breath. Well, that put her well and truly in her place. For the third time in as many minutes, she got to her feet. It was all too silly. She must resemble a jack-in-the-box: up, down, up again. A small smile tilted the corners of her mouth.

Not for long, however. For Alexander followed her lead and stood up also. 'If you've finished, we'll go back into the sitting room and discuss the work you've come here to do.'

Jamie stared at him, literally speechless.

'Nothing to say? Given your previous loquaciousness, you do surprise me.' He raised an eyebrow at her before saying, 'Yes, I've decided you can stay. I've really no alternative, a fact I'm sure you — and Adrian — were very well aware of.' He did manage a tight smile at that point. 'The truth is, there simply isn't the time to find another artist — not with the publishing deadline looming.'

3

When Jamie reached the hallway the following morning, the first thing she saw was the front door standing open to the brilliance of the morning sunshine; then she noticed a beautiful golden retriever lying across the entrance, pale head resting upon front paws, for all the world as if waiting for someone.

'Hello, boy — or is it girl?' Jamie exclaimed. 'Aren't you gorgeous?' She'd had no notion that Alexander owned a dog. But the knowledge that he did made him seem a little more human, a little less intimidating. She held out a cautious hand, not moving any closer to the animal until she discovered precisely how it was going to react to her unfamiliar presence in the house.

She needn't have worried, however. The dog got to its feet and walked towards her, its tail moving from side to side, its inky eyes not leaving her. It was as if the gentle gaze was weighing her up before finally deciding she was someone to be trusted. The dog reached her and thrust its nose into her hand, nuzzling her affectionately.

'I see you've met Sophie.' A beaming Mrs Skinner bustled into the hallway. 'My word,' she cried, taking in the sight of Sophie's unmistakable acceptance of Jamie, 'she's taken a shine to you and no mistake. I'm amazed. Other than with Miss Francesca, she's usually a bit stand-offish — even with my Dennis, who she's known since she was a puppy.'

Jamie glanced up at her from where she was bending over the dog, stroking her. 'She was Francesca's — Mrs Whittaker's dog?'

'Oh, my Lord, yes. Thought the sun shone out of Miss Francesca, she did. The day she disappeared, Sophie almost went crazy. She's waited at that door every morning since. Miss Francesca took her out at this time, you see. It's heartbreaking to watch, it really is. She waits here again each evening. That was her second walk of the day — the final one with Ms Francesca. Mr Xander always took her late at night. My Dennis has been walking her ever since . . . ' The older woman's words faded as emotion overwhelmed her.

Jamie crouched down so that her eyes were on a level with Sophie's. 'You poor, poor thing.'

The dog responded to the murmuring words by licking her face.

'Well, I never did,' Mrs Skinner said. 'She hasn't looked this way since before . . . before . . . ' Once more, it was as if she couldn't say the words: 'Miss Francesca disappeared'. She did gaze curiously, almost speculatively, at Jamie, however.

Jamie hurriedly straightened. Was it possible that Sophie somehow knew she was her beloved mistress's sister? Could a dog, with its acute sense of smell, associate one person with another? If so, she'd have to be careful. Sophie could be the one, albeit in complete innocence, to give her away.

'Do you think Sophie would come out with me this morning?' Jamie asked, in an attempt to distract the housekeeper's attention from the sight of Sophie nuzzling her legs with her wet nose. 'She could show me the moors, stop me from getting hopelessly lost.' Jamie smiled. 'Living here, she must be familiar with them. I've got some sketching to do.'

'I'm sure she would. It would be company for you.'

So, lifting the bag containing her sketching materials onto her shoulder, Jamie left the house. Sophie bounded ahead, impatient to stretch her legs, yet every now and again pausing in her run to look back and wait for Jamie to catch her up.

The evening before, Alexander had made it very clear to Jamie that he demanded work of the highest calibre from the artists he employed — original work taken from life and sketches, not copies reproduced from other books or photographs. 'If I wanted work that resembled a photograph then that's what I would use,' he'd told her.

'Could you give me some idea of which subjects in particular you're looking for?' Jamie had nervously asked.

It had to be said, Alexander's manner had been brusque. Was he already regretting that he'd agreed to her staying? Because if that was the case, then it would make her task even harder than it already was looking — I mean, sketching birds as they moved. It would be well nigh impossible. As it was, she suspected he'd be looking for fault in anything she presented to him — simply because she was a woman.

'I've prepared a list for you — which I hope will be helpful, as you aren't familiar with British wildlife.' He handed her a couple of sheets of paper. 'It covers all the birds I want to feature. It's got the smallest, such as the tit family — wrens, the goldcrest if you're very lucky; they're rather shy — right up to larger birds of prey such as buzzards; maybe a peregrine falcon — again, only if you're lucky; sparrow hawks. Then there are the birds that one associates with rivers: kingfishers, herons, dippers, and curlews. After that come the animals: deer, badger, fox, wild mink, otters, and rabbits, of course.'

If he was trying to intimidate her, he was succeeding. Jamie drew a breath and nervously interrupted, 'And if I don't see all the specimens that you've mentioned?'

He shrugged. 'Well then, I'll have to manage without. These have to be paintings taken from life, as I've said, so everything depends on luck and you being in the right place at the right time.'

Feeling a little better at that, she asked, 'Do the herds of ponies still roam?'

His one eyebrow lifted, denoting surprise, she assumed. 'You've heard of them then, have you? Yes, they're still around. Not in the numbers that they used to be, but you should see them. I've included them on my list, naturally.' He paused. 'A word of warning — you'll need to watch out for boggy ground.'

'Boggy ground?' she gasped.

'Yes, there are a few places that could be dangerous to the unwary. Also, a couple of the larger rivers are extremely fast-flowing, so try not to fall in.' He gave a glimmer of a smile as he handed over the sheets of paper.

Jamie was convinced at that juncture that he was being deliberately provocative. Well, she wasn't going to give him the satisfaction of rising to it. She certainly wouldn't show the fear that suddenly pierced her. So when he smoothly asked if she had any questions, she replied equally smoothly, 'I can't think of any.' She glanced down at the list he'd given her, somehow managing to hide her horror at the extent of the demands he was placing on her. 'I think you've pretty well covered everything.'

She was, however, wondering just how long he was expecting her to stay here, because the list, at first glance, looked quite impossible to fulfil in anything under two to three months. What about the publisher's deadline? 'I'll need to mug up on some of the birds you've mentioned, of course, to enable me to recognise them. And possibly on a few of the animals too.' In reality, she didn't think she'd recognise many of them. 'Um — didn't David manage to complete any paintings?'

'A few, yes. But I prefer my books to be illustrated by just one artist, not several. You'll find plenty of reference books on the shelves in the sitting room. Take whichever of them you need.'

So that was what she did. She picked out three of them and took them up to her room with her, intending to study them closely before going to sleep. She was determined to prove to Alexander Whittaker that she was every bit as capable as any man, if it was the last thing she ever did.

The trouble was, things didn't quite pan out as she had hoped. The events of the evening, added to her fairly long journey to Devon, had so tired her that long before she'd even got through the first of the books, her eyes had closed. She woke in the early hours of the morning to find her bedside lamp still on and the book that she had been studying lying upside-down on her chest. She did manage, then, to swiftly search for several of the birds and animals he'd mentioned and take some photographs on her mobile phone of the pictures shown.

This ensured that her first day upon the moor proved relatively productive, and it was with a dozen or so sketches completed that she decided to head back to Moorlands. Despite Alexander's warning against replicating photographs, she had taken some because, as far as the birds were concerned, it had proved almost impossible to sketch them in any real detail. They moved around far too quickly, fluttering through trees and hedgerows, never still for longer than a second or two. She'd take care that she didn't simply reproduce the photos though; it was the physical details of each bird that she needed.

She gazed down at the dog sitting quietly at her side. She smiled fondly at her, and gently caressed the silky ears. 'Time for home, eh, Sophie?'

As if she understood, Sophie got to her feet and wagged her tail. Jamie squinted up at the sun, belatedly seeing how low it was in the sky. The shadows were already beginning to lengthen. She checked her watch. Seven thirty. Later than she'd realised. There was a fair way to go to reach the house; too far, she guessed. It was almost the end of August, so it wouldn't be long before it was starting to get dark. The memory of Alexander's voice warning her of the bogs that dotted Dartmoor rang in her ears, quickening her heartbeat and inducing a feeling of alarm. With the light fading, she could be in one before she even realised it was there.

'Come on, girl,' she said to Sophie. 'Let's have a run, shall we?' The dog barked as if she understood every word, and Jamie's step quickened until it was a fast trot.

Which proved a huge mistake.

Sophie, taking her cue from the sound of Jamie's urgency, broke into a fast run, bounding through the tapestry of purple heather and larger clumps of a buttery yellow flower — so fast that one minute she was there, the next she'd gone. Jamie ran to the top of the slope over which the dog had disappeared and gazed anxiously around. But trees and dense hedgerows obscured her view, ensuring there was no sign of Sophie. 'Sophie,' she called, 'come here — to me. Good dog, Sophie . . . ' But it was no use.

She ran on then, desperate to find the animal. But in the swiftly gathering dusk, and no matter how far she went, she didn't catch a single glimpse of

Sophie. She called one last time — in vain. The animal had vanished, leaving no trace behind her. There was also, Jamie belatedly realised, no trace of any of the landmarks she'd taken such careful note of on the way out: the various granite tors and outcroppings that she'd passed and which the moors were known for; a lone wind-stunted tree. At one point there'd been a dry stone wall, she recalled.

There was no sign of any of it.

Eventually she came to a halt, panting and exhausted. Bending forward, she rested her hands on her knees as she fought for breath as well as calm. Her heart thudded in her breast as she realised she was hopelessly lost.

Telling herself not to panic, as that would be the worst thing she could do, she trudged onwards, her gaze searching for anything she could recognise; anything remotely familiar. Why on earth hadn't she thought to bring a map with her?

Then, all of a sudden, there was the

stunted tree, and nearby the monolithic stone tor that she had taken particular note of. That meant she must be a couple of miles at least from the house. Another forty-five minutes of walking, she estimated. Just enough time before total darkness fell.

With that worry out of the way, other more disturbing questions made their presence felt. Questions like, what was Alexander going to say when she returned without Sophie? She'd considered calling him, but as she hadn't entered his phone number into her own phone and foolishly hadn't brought the piece of paper she'd originally written it down on with her, that was out of the question. In any case, when she checked her phone there was no signal here, in the middle of nowhere.

The sun was little more than a sliver of gold above the horizon when she finally saw the silhouette of Moorlands looming up before her. Every window was illuminated so that the house was a blaze of light. Breathing a silent prayer of thanks, she headed towards it. It was then that she heard the sound of a dog barking.

'Sophie,' she breathed in relief, just as a furry body launched itself at her, practically knocking her over. 'Thank goodness. You naughty girl.'

At the same moment exactly, a second much larger and considerably more intimidating form appeared behind Sophie. A form that, with a sinking heart, Jamie had no trouble recognising.

'Where the blazes have you been?' Alexander's voice raged at her. 'You stupid, thoughtless woman. I was just coming out to look for you.'

4

'I'm sorry,' Jamie managed to stammer through the anger she was experiencing at the way he was speaking to her. Anyone would think she'd deliberately lost her way, simply to annoy him. 'I was lost. When Sophie ran off, I made the mistake of chasing after her and completely lost my bearings.'

'When Sophie ran off,' Alexander furiously broke in, 'you should have returned to the house immediately. Have you any notion of what everyone thought when she turned up here alone? When it then began to get dark and you still hadn't arrived, the entire household descended into uproar. Mrs Skinner was just about to notify the police.'

Jamie tilted her head back and looked up into eyes that had darkened from amber to the exact shade of treacle toffee — except for the minute gold flecks, that was, and they were blazing every bit as brightly as the windows of the house behind him. His expression would have been quite capable of blistering paint if there'd been any around.

'I didn't know she'd return to the house.' Oh God, how lame did that sound? Of course Sophie would return home. Where else would she go? If Jamie hadn't been in such a panic, she'd have thought of that herself.

'Well, of course she'd return to the house,' Alexander echoed her thoughts exactly, 'if she lost sight of you. What else was she supposed to do? And that was well over an hour ago, apparently.'

'Apparently?'

'So Mrs Skinner informed me. I've only just returned myself. I've been out too. If I'd been here, believe me, young lady, you'd have been found and brought home there and then.'

He was treating her like he would a naughty child. He was also being totally unreasonable. He knew she would probably have gone out to sketch. He was the one who'd told her to go out and about, for goodness sake.

But it was more than evident that Alexander Whittaker was in no mood to be reasonable. 'Do me a favour in future, will you? Either take an ordnance map with you, or stick to the path that you took on the way out. Women,' he ground out through tightly compressed lips. 'This is exactly what I expected.' And with that he strode back into the house, his face ashen with fury still, leaving Jamie staring after him, eyes wide with dismay.

She gnawed at her bottom lip. How could she have been so stupid? She'd unwittingly confirmed his low opinion of women in general. 'Oh dear, Sophie. What have we done?'

Jamie regarded the dog who, after her master's blistering attack, now looked every bit as dejected as she herself felt. The dog's tail drooped. She seemed to know that she'd been every bit as much in the wrong as Jamie. It didn't help to admit that Alexander was right. She shouldn't have rushed off in what had turned out to be a futile pursuit of the animal. She should have returned to Moorlands straight away, guessing that Sophie would instinctively head for home.

However, that admission in no way lessened her indignation at the way he'd spoken to her. A few simple words of reproach would have been sufficient. She sighed. It didn't augur well for their working relationship if that was the way he intended to behave each time something displeased him. Maybe she should give in to the inevitable and accept defeat; simply pack her bag and go.

But a determination to prove him wrong told her: no. She wasn't one to give up on things just because they didn't go as she wanted straight away.

'Come on, girl,' she said to Sophie. 'It looks as if we're sharing the same doghouse. We may as well get into it.'

As she entered the house, Mrs Skinner hurried over to her. 'Now, miss, don't you let Mr Xander upset you. He didn't know what he was saying.'

'You heard, then?'

'It would have been difficult not to.' She gave a small smile. 'I want to explain something to you. It might make you think a little better of Mr Xander.' She hesitated as if unsure whether or not to go on. 'The afternoon Miss Francesca disappeared — well, Sophie came back alone then too. The only difference, as you now know, between that occasion and this . . . ' She paused again, clearly in some distress. Jamie knew what she was about to say. 'Well, we never did see Miss Francesca again.'

★　★　★

The following morning, Jamie nervously ventured downstairs for breakfast to be greeted by Brad saying, 'What's this I've been hearing about your adventure yesterday? You caused ructions here, it seems.'

He gave a loud laugh. 'Especially as Xander was nowhere to be found either. He was out the afternoon Francesca went missing too — did you know that? Coincidence, do you think?' he silkily asked. 'Or something more . . . sinister?'

'Why don't you just say what you mean, Brad?'

'Certainly. What I mean is that the last time a woman went missing from this house, practically the last person to be seen with her was Xander — according to a witness. It was believed at the time he'd done away with her. You must have read about it?' She nodded. 'The story made the papers worldwide. Caused quite a stir, as you can imagine. Almost as big a stir as you caused yesterday. Mrs Skinner was all for calling the police.'

'So I heard. But . . . ' She frowned at him. 'You can't seriously believe your own brother had anything to do with his wife's disappearance? The police obviously didn't. They released him with no charges.'

'Don't be misled by that. My dear brother has always been adept at getting himself off the hook.'

'But you don't really think Alexander killed her, do you?'

Brad shrugged. 'It's possible. Xander can be utterly ruthless when circumstances demand it. And Francesca had been making life somewhat difficult for him.'

'In what way?'

'Well, one complaint he had was her extravagance.'

'But she was a wealthy woman in her own right, wasn't she? At least,' she hurried on to explain, 'that's what I read. Her father left her all his money, didn't he?'

'Oh Lord, yes. She was a millionairess, by all accounts. Her account, mainly,' he drily added. 'She liked everyone to know how much she was worth. There was no sense of modesty about Francesca.'

Jamie disregarded his acid remarks. 'So what was the problem, as far as

Alexander was concerned? It was surely her own money she was spending.'

He regarded her with more than a little amusement. 'How innocent you are, my dear,' Brad scoffed.

Jamie stiffened. What was it with English men? First Rob tried to tell her what she should and shouldn't do. Then Alexander raged at her. All right, maybe he had some reason, but his reaction had still been way over the top. Now Brad was patronising her. Anyone would think she was a child again — and she was getting more than a little fed up with it.

'I know you've only just arrived, but surely Xander's behaviour since then has been demonstration enough of his chauvinism? I heard he practically turned you away on the doorstep.'

He'd heard? Who from? Or had he been somewhere eavesdropping? That seemed the only explanation. Mrs Skinner, she was sure, hadn't been around at the time of her arrival; and anyway, she'd looked genuinely surprised when she realised who Jamie was.

'The truth is, Xander couldn't bear people knowing how financially independent of him his wife was. He wanted a demure, stay-at-home wife; instead, he got Francesca.' He gave a snort of sardonic laughter. 'A thoroughly modern, high-spirited, wildly extroverted woman. And with the benefit of her inheritance, the last thing she needed to be was dependent on or accountable to a husband. She didn't need Xander, and she made no secret of it. That's what stuck in his craw. Between you and me,' he added, leaning towards her and affecting a conspiratorial manner, 'Xander was the last thing she needed — or wanted.'

Jamie pulled away; he was getting too close for comfort.

'Well,' Brad said with a sly glance, 'not to beat about the proverbial bush, but my sister-in-law liked variety. In her life and her men.'

'What proof do you have of that?' Jamie hotly demanded.

'Well, none,' Brad drawled, 'but she used to tell me things — things she wouldn't want anyone else to know. No, the truth is Xander wanted shot of her. An opportunity came and he grabbed it.' He eyed her. 'Is all this talk making you nervous? You look a bit pale about the gills.'

'Why on earth should it? As I've already said, nothing's ever been proved against Alexander, has it?' Brad shook his head. 'And if what you're implying about Francesca is true, then who's to say that she simply hasn't run off with another man?'

'Leaving everything behind her?' Brad scoffed. 'All her money untouched? That's not Francesca's way. She'd have taken it all with her. Besides, what about the earring that was found — you do know about that?'

She nodded. 'It was found at somewhere called Cromer Pool.'

'That's right. The place where she was seen — with someone who looked very much like Xander. My guess is there was a struggle and it was pulled from her ear. It all points to murder — of the most foul,' he went on with more than a touch of melodrama. 'And despite all that he says, in my book, my dear brother is suspect numero uno. After all, don't they say, 'If in doubt, look at the husband?'

It almost sounded as if Brad wanted the guilty person to be Alexander and, moreover, wanted Francesca to be dead. Could he be right? Was she dead? A spasm of anguish pierced Jamie at the most likely answer to that. 'Did someone actually identify the man with her as Alexander?' she went on to ask.

'Yes.'

'They saw his face?'

Brad shrugged.

'Well, if the witness didn't see his face, it seems to me that there isn't any real proof that it was Alexander. It could simply be a case of mistaken identity. It wouldn't be the first time that that's happened. Anyway, where is this Cromer Pool?'

'About a mile or so from here. You might have passed it yesterday on your ramble.'

'No, I didn't pass any pools. At least, if I did, I didn't notice it.'

'Well, if you head more or less north east from the house, you can't miss it. Go along and have a look. It's a very pretty spot. Be sure you don't fall in though. It's said to be fairly deep. As kids, we believed it was bottomless. Not true, of course.'

At that point, Alexander strode into the room and the conversation was abruptly terminated, leaving Jamie feeling uncomfortable and more than a little anxious. Could Alexander have overheard their conversation?

★ ★ ★

The next day Jamie again ventured out onto the moors. This time, though, she took the precaution of walking into the nearby village and purchasing a detailed map of the area. She didn't intend to get lost again.

She swiftly located Cromer Pool on it and headed off in that direction. It didn't look that far away, a mile maybe. Sophie was with her once again. The dog had barely left her side since she'd run off the day before. It was as if she feared Jamie's disappearance too. In fact, Jamie was beginning to suspect that she had replaced her sister in the animal's affections — which made her wonder how Sophie would react to her eventual departure.

The other thing that bothered her was someone else questioning the dog's sudden devotion to a woman who, until a couple of days before, had been a stranger. Was it likely that they would put two and two together and arrive at the right answer? Not least because if they really looked at her, there was an unmistakable similarity between the sisters; they had the same eyes, the same hair. Anyone looking at the portrait of Francesca and then looking at Jamie right afterwards surely couldn't fail to see the likeness. And if that should happen, how would she explain her duplicity to Alexander? It didn't bear thinking about. She was sure it would make his rage the previous evening look like chicken feed in comparison.

Maybe she should come clean to him; admit who she was? But that could make it even harder to continue with her investigation into her sister's disappearance. Her confession would be bound to influence everyone; influence what they felt able to say about the missing woman in her presence. No, she had to carry on as she was, an unknown artist here simply to work. It was her only chance of finding out what had happened to Francesca.

And that was becoming increasingly important to Jamie. So much so, in fact, that nothing else really mattered.

* * *

After a fairly tense dinner the evening before, Jamie had pleaded exhaustion and gone to her room. A low whining outside her door sometime later had led her to open it, whereupon she discovered Sophie outside, with such a pleading and utterly pathetic look to her that Jamie was helpless to resist.

'In you come,' she'd said, standing to one side. The dog had bounded in, to immediately position herself on the floor at the side of the bed, where she stretched out, her head resting on her front paws, before closing her eyes.

Jamie smiled as she climbed into bed. And the truth was that Sophie's presence throughout the night induced such a sense of security within her that she slept right through, untroubled for once by her theories and suspicions of what had happened to her sister.

They'd only been walking for half an hour or so when she spotted the sheen of water ahead. Cromer Pool? She consulted her map and confirmed that it was. Without a second's hesitation, she strode to the edge of it and stood looking down into the murky water. It wasn't a large pool, about a hundred metres across. It did, however, look very deep. Bearing in mind Brad's warning, she cautiously leant forward to stare down into the inky depths. She saw nothing other than her own reflection.

A stray breeze ruffled the water, breaking up her image, making her look momentarily like someone else. Another woman. A woman with waxy skin and huge, luminous eyes. A woman who lay just beneath the surface.

Francesca.

Jamie gasped and pulled back. She began to shiver. Her imagination was taking over, making her visualise things that weren't there.

She remembered the portrait of Francesca: the one that hung in such a prominent position in the sitting room; the one that wherever she sat, she could see; the one whose eyes followed her wherever she moved. Whatever her faults, there was a haunting beauty to her sister, with her creamy complexion and her enviable figure. Her cascade of honey-blonde hair was an exact match for Jamie's, as were her almost violet eyes.

A sense of melancholy overwhelmed Jamie then. Had all that loveliness been simply snuffed out? Brad thought so. She shuddered again, deathly cold despite the warmth of the morning. She hugged herself with both arms, still staring into the bleakly grey depths. There was barely any reflection in the water now, not even her own. It took Sophie's crying to drag her thoughts away from the sinister-looking pool and the image of Francesca that had appeared fleetingly before her.

'Sophie.' She dropped to her knees. The dog was trembling just as much as she was. 'What is it, Soph?'

Had the dog seen something the day her mistress disappeared? Something bad that she had come to associate with the pool?

'Come on, let's go. This isn't a good place to be for either of us. I'm beginning to see things that aren't there, and you . . . Well, I'm wondering if you've already seen things you shouldn't have.'

5

Surprisingly, in the wake of her disturbing visit to Cromer Pool, Jamie managed to complete several more sketches, and felt sufficiently confident about them the following morning to show them to Alexander. She had spread them out on the dining-room table for him to inspect. She wanted his approval and subsequent go-ahead before she made a start on the final paintings.

He leant over them, examining them closely for several minutes before finally straightening to look at Jamie and say, 'These are just what I'm looking for.' He paused. 'I think I owe you an apology.'

'Do you?' She felt sufficiently emboldened by his praise to look him straight in the eye. Was he going to apologise for his angry attack upon her the other evening? It seemed unlikely. Alexander Whittaker didn't strike her as being the sort of man to make any sort of concession regarding previous actions or words. Yet, he was about to apologise.

However, he didn't say anything at all for a moment. Instead, he continued to stare at her, a darkening of his eyes the only indication that he was in any way affected by her direct gaze. But even as she watched, the tiny gold flecks appeared, restoring the pupils to the amber colour that they usually were. She had deduced by now that they only appeared when he was emotionally moved — whether by anger or pleasure she had yet to fathom. She had an uncomfortable suspicion that it was anger, although that measure couldn't be applied this time. He was quite definitely pleased. This verdict was confirmed by the smile that was tilting the corners of his mouth.

It was the first time she'd seen him smile, and the difference the expression made to him was incredible. His face warmed, the usually harsh lines softening, and she was belatedly visited by the image of him bending his head forward to kiss her. Completely helpless against the sudden kick of passion that this thought engendered, she lowered her gaze and fixed it upon that unexpectedly sensual mouth.

'Jamie?'

Her face flamed as she lifted her gaze once more to meet his. The quality of his smile had changed. It was now one of quizzical amusement.

Oh God. She gnawed at her bottom lip, a sure sign of her confusion and embarrassment. How much of that unexpected surge of emotion had her expression revealed?

'What is it? What's wrong?' he gently asked.

Yes, he'd definitely picked up on her fleeting spasm of desire. 'Um — nothing,' she stammered. 'I was daydreaming.'

Would he accept this vague statement? Hopefully, if he did, it would allay any suspicions he might be having about her emotional response to him, given that fiery and revealing blush. 'You were going to say?' she went on, desperate to restore things to how they'd been before her wild imaginings.

'I was going to say,' he began — his eyes still hadn't left her face, which was disconcerting to say the least — 'that you're an excellent artist. Your sketches, as basic as they are at this stage, demonstrate that. David couldn't have bettered them. Take these two, for example. You've captured their colour and movement perfectly.' He picked up the drawing of the two kingfishers. There'd only actually been one but, in a surge of artistic licence, she'd drawn two. It had worked. 'They've come alive on the paper. And these ponies.' He lifted another sketch. 'Marvellous. Again, they're lively, full of movement. I take back everything I've ever said about women artists.' He glanced back at her, clearly expecting her to respond.

She didn't disappoint, though his frank admission that he'd been wrong in his bias coming this quickly, far more quickly than she'd anticipated, had astonished her.

'Thank you, Alexander — um, Xander.' She smiled up at him, something she also hadn't done till now. They'd previously spent the better part of their time together indulging in a mild form of sparring, mainly because Jamie constantly felt she needed to live up to his notions of what she should be: namely, a man. As a consequence, she'd suppressed her natural femininity.

So, for the first time in his company, she relaxed — began to think of him as Xander rather than Alexander, and it showed. Mainly in the way her violet eyes shone and her mouth softened.

Xander's eyes swept over her, from her smiling lips down. They seemed to caress her, making her glad for once of her curves, over-generous as she usually considered them. Roses warmed her cheeks, drawing his glance back to them. Twin dimples readily revealed themselves. His gaze lingered on her mouth, a mouth that just seconds ago had been smiling, but was now visibly trembling.

He took a step towards her, making her believe that the same sorts of emotions were assailing him. Especially when his voice was husky as he asked, 'What is it? Tell me.'

Jamie felt her breath catch in her throat as he closed the remaining gap between them. She was convinced he was about to hold her, kiss her. Her head tilted backwards as her lips parted in anticipation; her lids lowered over eyes that must be vivid with desire, with an expectation she was powerless to conceal.

He started to stretch his one hand out to her, but even as she lifted her own hand expectantly and waited for his touch, he took a step backwards, and she knew she'd made the most horrendous mistake. As if sensing that things were about to be transformed between them, instead of pulling her into his arms as she'd anticipated

— longed for, in fact — he'd turned away, his features hardening, a muscle in his jaw flexing.

Even worse than all of this, his voice had reverted to the wrong side of cool as he brusquely said, 'These sketches are fine.' He picked up the sheets of paper and began to stack them together. 'Perhaps you could begin on the final paintings tomorrow and we'll see how they shape up.'

To Jamie, who was still quivering with heightened emotion, his unexpected but unmistakable withdrawal was like a slap in the face. Nothing had changed, whatever she'd sensed beginning between them in those few moments. How naive of her. But what was much worse was the fact that she'd been on the verge of making an utter fool of herself. He couldn't have missed the fact that she'd all but offered herself to him — and he'd turned her down, unequivocally. Well, it would never happen again — no, sir. She'd treat him with the same sort of detachment that he showed her.

Swiftly, Xander divided the sketches into two piles. His hands were perfectly steady, Jamie saw. Unlike hers, which were still quivering. He indicated the smaller pile. 'I'd like these to be done in oils, the rest in watercolours.'

'Very well. Which would you like me to start on? The watercolours will be quicker.' Her tone had lost every vestige of its previous warmth and pleasure, as had her eyes, but Xander gave no indication that he noticed.

'Yes, do those first. I want to see what your finished work will be like.'

He began to move towards the door. He clearly couldn't wait to get away. Well, Jamie fumed, far be it from her to stop him. Her tone was as brusque as his had been as she said, 'Right. Watercolours it will be.'

Just as he was about to open the door, he turned back to her. 'By the way, Adrian Bryant is coming down next week. Monday or Tuesday, he wasn't sure which. He'll be confirming. I'd like a sample of both mediums to show him. You'll find materials in my studio should you need them. Feel free to use anything — the room as well. I won't be needing it this week.'

'Thank you, I've brought everything I'll need but I will use your studio.'

For a second, he seemed to hesitate as if about to say something else, but all he did was nod his head right before he strode from the room. It was as if he had a battalion of devils at his heels instead of just her.

Well, he needn't worry. She'd got the message and she wouldn't be making the same mistake again. She'd complete the tasks she'd come to do. The painting and, hopefully, the quest for whatever had happened to her sister would prove successful. And then she'd leave forthwith.

She picked up the twin piles of sketches, intending to go to the studio that Xander had said she could use. She'd better make a start on the first lot of paintings if all she had was a few days before Adrian was due.

She blindly strode from the room, only to walk straight into someone coming the other way. 'For heaven's sake, watch where you're going, will you?' a haughty but nonetheless attractively husky voice said. And Jamie found herself looking into a pair of the greenest eyes she'd ever seen. They were almost emerald.

'I'm terribly sorry. I didn't see you,' Jamie said.

'That was more than evident. Do you always leave a room at a gallop? If so, I'll have to watch out in the future.' The woman touched her long, satin-smooth blonde hair before brushing some sort of imaginary dirt from her trim but very shapely bosom — as if physical contact with Jamie had in some way contaminated her. 'Who are you, anyway? I didn't know Xander had a guest — other than the artist chappie, James somebody or other.'

'Jamie; it's Jamie, and that's me.'

'What?' The woman looked confused. 'What's you?'

'The artist chappie — that's me.'

'Oh, puh-*lease*. I might be accused now and then of not noticing the better part of the human race, but not even I could mistake you for a man. Or . . . ' She frowned then. 'Are you in some sort of drag?' She stared meaningfully at Jamie's voluptuous breasts and, not for the first time, Jamie found herself wishing they weren't such a prominent feature of her anatomy.

'No, I'm not in some sort of drag.' She couldn't help her indignation at such an outrageous assumption. 'I am a woman. It was a misunderstanding, confusion over my name.'

'I see.' She was intently studying Jamie now, her eyes narrowed with speculation. 'Don't I know you?'

Jamie stiffened but managed to keep her voice light and untroubled as she answered, 'I wouldn't think so. I'm only just over from Florida, where I've lived for the past twenty-one years. I'm Jamie Rivers.' She thrust out a hand, attempting a conciliatory smile as she did so, only to have it fall onto decidedly stony ground.

'Did Xander know you were a woman when he agreed to your coming?'

'No. As I said, it was a bit of a misunderstanding.'

'Oh boy.' Surprising her then, the woman laughed. 'Wouldn't I have loved to be here when you turned up. What did he say?'

Jamie couldn't help but laugh too. 'Let's just say he wasn't pleased.'

'I can imagine.' The other woman finally grasped Jamie's still-outstretched hand. 'I'm Rosamund Matthews, a neighbour of Xander's. His wife, Francesca, was a close friend. Did you know her?'

Jamie noted the use of the word 'was' in relation to her sister. Someone else who believed her dead?

'No, I'm afraid I didn't. As I said, I've only just recently arrived from Flor — '

'So you did.'

Jamie wondered then if Rosamund was trying to catch her out. Didn't she believe that Jamie had only just arrived in England? Or, more significantly, had she noted the resemblance to Francesca, but just hadn't realised it? A curl of apprehension began within Jamie as Rosamund continued to stare at her.

'I'm sure we've met somewhere. Are you positive that . . . ?'

'Positive.' Jamie's unease was intensifying. She had to get away from her. Thank heavens they weren't in the sitting room, because one look at the portrait of Francesca might be all it took for Rosamund to come up with the truth.

'I've never been to Florida, so it can't have been there. Oh well, it'll probably come to me eventually, because I'd put money on us having met.'

'Look, I must get on,' Jamie said. 'Work to do. Um, was it Alexander you wanted?'

'Yes,' the other woman purred. 'I'm doing my bit at consoling the poor, poor man. But he knows I'm coming so there's no need to find him and tell him.'

I wasn't going to, Jamie mentally told

her as she walked away. So she was consoling 'poor, poor' Xander, was she? Alexander Whittaker hadn't struck Jamie as needing any sort of consolation. For a man whose wife had vanished under mysterious circumstances, he was bearing up all too well — which did seem to lend the general assumption of his guilt rather more substance than she was comfortable with. Mind you, Francesca had disappeared a little over a year ago — so she supposed, to be fair, it was reasonable that he should be making a new life for himself.

She walked towards Xander's study, a feeling of misgiving beginning within her. Maybe it might be best to keep out of Rosamund's way. The last thing she needed was to be recognised as Francesca's sister.

★ ★ ★

Later that afternoon, she was on her way from the studio to her own bedroom when she passed a door standing partially open. Up until then it had always been closed, so she had no idea whose room it was. It was quite a distance from her own bedroom.

Could it be Xander's?

A furtive peek inside told her that it wasn't; that it must be Francesca's. It couldn't be mistaken for anything other than a woman's room, with its decor of apricot and lemon, and occasional touches of apple-green. There was no indication that Xander had shared it with her. Separate bedrooms?

Intrigued now, she took a step inside. She didn't feel she was snooping. Francesca had been her sister, after all, even though they'd had no contact in twenty-one years. And hadn't she come here to try and discover what had happened to her? In which case, it was perfectly excusable to explore every avenue that she could.

A hurried glance over her shoulder told her that no one was about; so, greatly daring, she walked further in.

The first thing to catch her eye was another, even larger, portrait of Francesca. Jamie walked across to it and stood beneath it, looking up. She'd been so beautiful; no wonder men had wanted her. 'Had'? Was she also assuming her sister was dead?

She shivered and turned away. Belatedly, she felt like an intruder. Despite what she had told herself, she had no right to be in here. She'd turned, preparing to leave the room, when a photograph on the dressing table snagged her attention.

She went across and lifted it up, her heartbeat quickening. She was looking at Xander standing at his wife's side on their wedding day. He was looking down at her, his pride in and love for the woman at his side only too apparent.

Feeling increasingly like some sort of voyeur, she replaced it; but then, quite unable to help herself, she pulled open the top drawer. Inside, nestled amongst the usual paraphernalia of a woman's dressing-table drawer, was a single emerald and diamond drop earring. The one found at the scene of the imagined crime? With quivering fingers, she picked it up. It was truly magnificent and, from the size and perfection of the emerald, probably worth a great deal of money. Carefully, she replaced it in the exact position that it had been in before she'd touched it.

A swift search of the lower drawers revealed only underwear, glamorous and made of silk, in every colour she could think of. Driven by a conviction that somewhere here she would find some sort of clue to her sister's whereabouts, Jamie next went to the set of wardrobes. They lined the whole of one wall. Ornately carved doors slid back at a touch, and inside were rows of exquisitely made garments.

Jamie's shoulders sagged. Brad had to be right. Francesca must be dead. No woman would leave home and not take at least some of these beautiful things. But nothing had been removed;

that was evident by the lack of any space on the rails. She glanced down at the neatly ordered rows of shoes. Again, no gaps.

'What the hell do you think you're doing?'

6

Jamie spun around to find herself facing Xander. He was standing mere inches behind her. That was fright enough, but what truly terrified her was the look of him. His eyes were blazing, his expression one of accusation and what looked dangerously like contempt.

And no wonder. What must he be thinking of her? Sneaking into his missing wife's room and then systematically going through her possessions — it was inexcusable.

'I'll ask you again. What are you doing in here?' And he reached out and grabbed hold of her shoulders.

'I'm sorry, I saw the open door and I . . . I . . . ' Jamie limped into silence. What could she say? There were no excuses for what she'd done. At least, not in Xander's eyes.

His top lip curled. 'And you just

couldn't resist a peek,' he finished for her. 'What did you expect to find? A body? A clue to where she is? What?' His hold on her tightened as his eyes narrowed. 'Or is it a more personal involvement than mere macabre nosiness? Did you know my wife?'

Jamie stared at him, her eyes wide with distress. Here was the opportunity to confess — but the fact that he looked like a stranger all of a sudden, and a threatening stranger at that, stopped her even as the words formed in her throat. How would he react if she told him of her deception? Would he physically harm her? After all, what did she really know of him; what he would be capable of in extreme circumstances? Especially if he was the one responsible for Francesca's disappearance? After all, everyone else thought he was — even the police at one juncture.

'No,' she stammered.

His eyes narrowed at her, his suspicion plain to see. 'You've shown a great deal of interest in her for someone who professes not to know her.' His head had drawn closer to hers. His breath feathered her forehead. She could see the pores of his skin; smell the clean man-scent of him. Fool! She was a complete idiot. Had she given herself away? If he knew that Francesca had a younger sister, would he make the connection?

'I've seen you studying her portrait — the one in the sitting room, of course; not this one. I even overheard you questioning Brad at one point.'

So as she'd feared, he had overheard her conversation with his brother a couple of days before. His eyes were hooded now, his expression one of even deeper suspicion. If he should glance at Francesca's portrait, her deception would be revealed, and then what would he do? Her breath snagged in her throat.

His voice was low as he asked, 'Did you know her?'

'Did?' she gasped. 'Do you think she's dead as well?'

That was her biggest mistake. She knew it as soon as she saw his expression change. 'There you go again. You do know her, don't you? Is that why you're here? Or is it simply morbid curiosity? The thrill of being in the room of a woman who has vanished in mysterious circumstances; the thrill of touching her things? Is that it? Or perhaps you wanted a memento? Well, which is it?' He shook her as his rage took over, his fingers bruising on the tops of her arms.

'No!' Jamie tore herself from his grasp. This was exactly what she'd feared. To add to her misgiving, there was a look in his eyes that totally unnerved her. 'How dare you imply —?'

He was breathing as heavily as she was by this time. His eyes were aflame, their gold flecks glittering. 'You disgust me,' he finally rasped out, thrusting her from him.

'I didn't intend coming in — I'm sorry. I was going to close the door and move on, but . . . but . . . '

'Yes, but?' His gaze was a bleak one now.

'I saw the portrait and then the photograph on the dressing table.'

Xander went and picked up the photograph. His anger seemed to have disappeared. 'Happier times — when Francesca and I were . . . ' His voice tailed off, but his words contained such a wealth of bitterness and regret that Jamie instinctively moved towards him. Before she could reach him, however, he opened the top drawer of the dressing table and dropped the photograph inside. The metal frame clattered onto the contents. The earring? He slammed the drawer shut and swung once more to Jamie. She took a step backwards. It was a purely instinctive gesture but one that Xander saw.

'Oh, you needn't worry. You have nothing to fear from me — in spite of all the gossip, which I'm sure you've heard by now.'

'I'm not worried — or afraid.' And she wasn't, she belatedly acknowledged.

Xander wouldn't hurt her. All of a sudden, she knew that without a shadow of doubt.

A smile of pure amusement lit his handsome features then, as with a couple of purposeful strides he closed the gap between them. This time Jamie stood her ground, her small chin defiantly in the air as she held his gaze with her own.

He stood in front of her. 'Admirable,' he said. 'There's a great deal more to you than meets the eye, isn't there? I started to realise that this morning when I saw the quality of your work.' He lifted a hand and with his index finger tilted her chin even higher, so much so that her neck was bent back at a sharp, almost painful angle as she was compelled to look directly at him.

All Jamie could think was, he couldn't know how true his first words were, could he? There was a strange expression in his eyes, so maybe he did, and for his own purposes was allowing her to continue with her deception.

Defensively, she closed her eyes, shutting out his penetrating stare, so she didn't see his head moving down to hers. The first thing she knew was the grinding of his lips over hers. Her eyes sprang open and she found herself looking directly into the amber depths. But even as she watched him, his lids lowered, guarding his expression from her, as his hands slid around her waist, pulling her close and pinning her to him. Her breasts flattened against him as her thighs pressed themselves to his.

She gave a small sigh as, sliding her arms up his chest and around the back of his neck, she relinquished herself to his kiss. It was as if every bit of desire, every suppressed longing, was at last unleashed. As if this kiss had been destined from the very start.

She thought she felt the brush of his fingers against her breast, but as he pushed her from him at that very moment, she couldn't be sure. Perhaps it had simply been her own passion that had fuelled the sensation of his fingers so intimately upon her.

Nonetheless, if Jamie felt as if her every emotion, every nerve ending were exposed and quivering, Xander appeared completely unaffected. His cool glance told her nothing of his feelings at their lovemaking. Jamie braced herself for further recrimination, maybe even more contempt. After all, she had given in to him straight away; had made no attempt to free herself.

That recrimination didn't come, however. 'Ye-es,' Xander breathed, 'definitely more than meets the eye.' And with that, he strode from the room and she was alone once more. Jamie lay in bed that night quite unable to sleep. Images of Xander and the way she'd felt at his kiss were too vivid to allow her the relief of slumber. She was deeply attracted to him, she mutely agonised. How could she possibly be attracted to a man who everybody seemed to suspect had murdered her sister? It was unthinkable.

From that time on, Jamie made sure she gave the appearance of immersing herself totally and solely in her art. But she knew that the only solution to her dilemma was to find out what had happened to Francesca. Because something had — she was increasingly certain of that.

* * *

Xander was also hard at work preparing his next television series, as well as working on the manuscript for his book. As he was closely involved with the filming, which was taking place on Dartmoor, it meant he was hardly ever at home, which considering their last disturbing encounter was perhaps a good thing.

One afternoon, sorely lacking inspiration for her next painting — or even the will to pick up a brush — Jamie found Sophie and prepared herself for a long walk on the moors. There were several areas — near enough to walk to — that she hadn't yet explored. She would avoid Cromer Pool. She was in no mood for its air of bleak desolation.

She was heading for the front door, Sophie hugging her heels, when she heard Brad hailing her. 'Where are you two headed?'

'We're off for a walk. I thought maybe I'd find some inspiration on the moors. Um, you and Xander have a flat in London, don't you?' Lying in bed the night before, she had wondered if Francesca kept a separate store of clothes and possessions there. If so, what was to say she hadn't gone there and gathered some things together and then simply left?

'Xander does, yes.'

She hesitated. Would it be dangerous to show too much interest in her sister's whereabouts — especially if Xander heard about it? After all, he'd already caught her in his wife's bedroom. Oh, go for it, she decided. It was the only way to try and find out precisely what had happened in the run-up to her disappearance. And, after all, wasn't that why she was here?

'Did Francesca use it too?' she asked.

But Brad seemed to find nothing strange in the question. 'Yes, she did. Whenever she'd had enough of my brother. It gave her the chance to meet her . . . other friends too.'

'Did she keep any clothes there?'

'I think so. Why?'

'Oh, it's something that occurred to me.'

Brad made no pretence of not being interested in what she was about to say. 'What?'

'Well, everyone assumes that because she's taken nothing from here, it must point to harm having befallen her. But supposing she's taken belongings from the flat instead?'

Brad eyed her. 'Well, I'm sure the police checked that.' A gleam appeared in his eye. 'But I tell you what — as you're interested in the case, why don't you and I do a bit of detective work of our own, eh? We could go along and check out what's missing.' He moved closer to her, close enough for his breath to feather the skin of her face. 'What do you say? We could also get to know each other a little better.'

She couldn't miss his lustful expression. Surely he couldn't be mistaking her interest in Francesca's disappearance as a romantic interest in himself?

'Oh no, I didn't mean — '

'Then what did you mean, Jamie?' He slid an arm about her waist, pulling her in to him. She tried to free herself but he simply tightened his hold.

'Please, Brad. You're right, of course; the police would most certainly have checked that. Stupid of me to think otherwise.' She gave a small laugh.

A deep growl startled them both. She watched as Brad's expression was transformed from one of lust to that of intense irritation. He glanced down, as Jamie did, to see Sophie standing close, her hackles raised and her teeth bared as she stared up at Brad.

'Sophie!' Jamie cried. Such unbridled ferocity was totally out of character for the placid animal. However, she didn't feel she could condemn the dog's actions, for Brad released her instantly, muttering words that sounded like, 'Bloody dog. She wants teaching a lesson.'

As if she sensed the threat in Brad's demeanour, Sophie launched herself forward, to take hold of one of Brad's trouser legs with her teeth.

'Let go — damn you.' He tried to kick her off him but Sophie hung on, her only sound a deep-throated snarl. She began to shake the leg back and forth as if it were a rag doll.

For her part, Jamie could only stare at the dog. Whatever had come over her? The only explanation was that she must have deemed Brad a threat in some way. Deciding it was time she intervened, she commanded,' Sophie, let go.'

The animal did so immediately, but she continued to watch Brad closely.

'Why would she do that?' Jamie asked. 'She's so gentle, normally.'

Brad gave a snort and proceeded to lift his trouser leg and examine the skin beneath. Sophie's teeth marks were clearly visible, but she hadn't broken the skin. Brad straightened and chuckled. 'She came upon me and Francesca indulging in some horseplay one day that got a little out of hand. Sophie misread the situation, just as she has now, and ever since, she feels she has to bare her teeth at me now and again. It's all harmless fun. She wouldn't hurt me, would you, Soph?'

But the dog didn't respond to his affectionate glance. Jamie hid a smile. 'I don't think she agrees, Brad.'

'Oh, she's just playing.' And, in truth, now that Brad had moved away from Jamie, Sophie did seem to be regarding him more benignly.

'Um, what did you mean, Brad? Horseplay that got out of hand?'

'Sometimes I don't know my own strength, that's all. I made Francesca squeal. Mind you, she didn't usually object to a bit of fun.' His smile was a sly one. 'When Xander was out of the way, naturally.'

Was he implying that he and his sister-in-law had been having an affair? 'Didn't Francesca mind when you hurt her? It must have been a pretty dramatic squeal to have Sophie reacting so angrily.'

'She whinged a bit, but we were soon friends again. She needed me. I was her confidant. Poor thing had no one else. We are rather remote here.'

'I see. And yet Rosamund Matthews told me she and Francesca were close friends. Wouldn't Francesca have confided in her? You know, another woman?'

'Not likely,' he snorted. 'Rosamund knew Xander long before Francesca appeared on the scene. Her nose was well and truly knocked out of joint by Xander and Francesca's marriage. She's the last person Francesca would have confided in. She wouldn't have trusted her not to run straight to Xander with anything she told her. Between you and me, Francesca's vanishing act suits Rosamund extremely well. Playing the role of chief comforter, as she likes to describe herself, allows her to sink her claws back into Xander. She always had designs on him. In fact, I sometimes wonder whether she mightn't have encouraged Xander to get rid of Francesca.'

Brad's words provided Jamie with plenty to think about. If Francesca was indeed dead — which, even she had to admit, was looking increasingly likely — then it sounded as if it were Rosamund who had the greatest motive for getting rid of her. She wanted Xander for herself. But what if Xander had belatedly decided he wanted Rosamund? That would also be a pretty powerful motive. Especially as it sounded as if Francesca had regularly cheated on Xander. A man as proud as Xander looked to be wouldn't take kindly to being made a fool of.

★　★　★

By the next day, Jamie had decided to take her suspicions to the Plymouth constabulary. There being no local police force any longer, they were the ones who had investigated Francesca's disappearance, she'd discovered. There were a few questions she wanted answered, anyway.

Her luck was in because DI Durrant was there at the station; he was the plain-clothes detective who had headed the investigation. She had remembered his name from the newspaper reports and had asked to speak to him specifically.

'What can I do for you, Ms Rivers?' he asked once she'd finally managed to get in to see him.

'I'm staying at Moorlands.'

'Are you, now?' The man leant back into his chair, the fingers of his one hand tapping the desk behind which he sat. 'And what would you be doing there?'

'I'm working with Alexander Whittaker on the illustrations for his new book.'

He eyed her for a long moment. 'Did you know about Mrs Whittaker's disappearance and his arrest on suspicion of her murder when you agreed to come and work with him?'

'Yes.'

'And yet you still came?' Jamie nodded. 'Brave girl.'

'Not really. I never believed he had anything to do with Francesca's disappearance. He had too much to lose — his career, his fan base . . . even his wealth, ultimately.'

'I see.' He steepled his fingers beneath his chin. 'You seem very sure of that.'

'You released him, so . . . ' She shrugged.

'We had no choice. No body, no evidence against him of any sort. Ergo, no crime.'

'But what about the earring that was found at one of the last places she was seen?'

The inspector shrugged. 'It could have fallen off her ear. Women are notorious for losing the odd earring, aren't they?'

Jamie had no answer for that.

'If you don't mind me asking, Ms Rivers, why are you so interested in this case? I know you're working with Mr Whittaker, but your interest does seem inordinately intense.'

'Yes. That's because Francesca Whittaker was my sister, Inspector.'

7

'Was she, now? In that case, I can see why you're so interested.' He stared at her; there was more than a hint of suspicion in his gaze. 'But there's been no mention of a sister in all of our investigations.'

'No, there wouldn't have been.' She went on to explain why no one knew who she was and why she wished to stay incognito.

He still looked sceptical, however. 'Do you have some form of identification?'

Jamie showed him her passport, which she'd carried with her ever since her arrival in the UK.

'Thank you. Well, in that case, I can tell you what we know. We're treating the case as an ongoing missing person enquiry until substantial evidence turns up that a crime has actually been committed. At the moment, there is none. There were no signs of a struggle; no signs of a murder. And her passport was still at the house, so she can't have left the country.'

'But what about all her belongings? Wouldn't she have taken at least some of them if she simply ran away? Did you check the London flat?'

'Yes — well, the local police did.'

'And was everything that should have been there still there?'

'As far as they could tell, yes. Nothing looked to be obviously missing. Wardrobes were full, as were the drawers and cupboards. I believe Mr Whittaker has visited since then, and as he hasn't reported anything missing . . . ' He shrugged his shoulders.

'It's the same at Moorlands. But what woman would go, leaving every one of her possessions behind — some of them extremely valuable?'

'A woman who wants to make a quick getaway, perhaps with a lover. And it's not the first time, not by a mile, that people have disappeared under such circumstances. Why, we had one only last month; a woman vanished in a very similar manner. Took only the bare minimum — mind you, the husband hadn't a clue as to what was missing or not. The only difference was she turned up again last week. She had gone abroad; she'd been to Spain with a boyfriend. They fell out. She decided she'd been too rash and back she came. Husband took her back too.' He smiled at her. 'So you see, without some firm evidence of foul play and no body, there's not a lot we can do.

'We don't know what sort of relationship she and Mr Whittaker had. There's been no suggestion of any sort of abuse, but . . . ' He shrugged. 'If she wanted to disappear permanently and not have a possibly violent husband pursuing her, then it's not beyond belief that she deliberately contrived to make it look as if she'd been killed — which would explain her taking nothing with her. The earring strategically placed could certainly suggest that. Her car was also spotted that evening, with two people in it, a man and a woman.' He paused for a moment. 'The vehicle has never been found, which does seem to suggest that wherever she is, she has it with her.

'She wasn't drowned in Cromer Pool. We had frogmen down there and they found nothing. There wasn't a body; there was nothing there apart from weeds and a few fish.'

'But is all that you've said likely? I mean, does Alexander Whittaker seem like a violent man? I've not seen anything in him to suggest such a thing.' Jamie said. 'She was seen arguing with a man by the pool who a witness identified as possibly being Alexander. Would she run off just because she had a row with her husband, leaving everything she owned behind? And what if it wasn't Alexander? And if you truly believe she's disappeared of her own volition, then why are you still investigating?'

'Well, let's say we're keeping an open

mind, Ms Rivers. Plus, there's been pressure from Whittaker to keep the case open. He wants her found — to clear his name, I shouldn't wonder. Myself, I think she'll be back when she's bored with whoever she's with.'

Brad could be correct about her sister's affairs. The inspector sounded as if he was giving credence to that theory. Jamie went on to tell him what Brad had told her about Rosamund and her past, and possibly current, relationship with Alexander. 'I wondered if anyone had mentioned it to you?'

'Yes, Brad Whittaker did. He's been very helpful.'

'I believe the witness at the pool was a local person. Could you give me their name, Inspector? I'd really like to speak to whoever it was.'

★   ★   ★

Jamie climbed into her car and, consulting the piece of paper with the witness's name and address on it that the inspector had given her, she drove off.

'Your sister made a withdrawal of cash from her bank account the month before she went missing,' Durrant had told her. 'Enough to enable her to cover living expenses for some time. Not in the style to which she would have become accustomed, but I suppose if the man she's gone with is wealthy . . . ' He shrugged. ' . . . she wouldn't need her own money.'

'But even then,' Jamie argued, 'would she leave all she owned behind?'

Jamie wasn't so sure. It had been over twelve months now since Francesca had vanished. If she'd simply left Xander, wouldn't someone have spotted her by now, somewhere? Especially if she hadn't left the country. There'd been massive publicity at the time of her disappearance. It didn't add up; none of it did. Unless, of course, she'd managed to acquire a second passport. Was that possible? Jamie resolved to do some digging herself and see what she could come up with.

The village was only a small place with no more than half a dozen shops in all, but it was bustling with people and traffic. Jamie quickly located 6 Widecombe Road, the home of the witness who'd seen Francesca, and someone she'd identified as Xander, arguing. The woman's name was Pascoe.

'See if you can jog her memory for anything she might have forgotten at the time that I saw her, Ms Rivers.'

Jamie intended to try. She pulled onto a narrow, well-kept driveway and within seconds was ringing the doorbell of a pink-walled bungalow. An elderly woman opened the door almost at once, a small Yorkshire terrier at her heels. It immediately began to bark, and even the woman regarded Jamie with suspicion. Jamie hastily gave her name and told her the purpose of her visit.

'You'm not one of them press people, are you? 'Cause they didn't leave me alone for a while,' she said. Her faded blue eyes took on a definite sparkle as she spoke, however, so Jamie guessed, despite her words, that she'd rather enjoyed her brief spell of notoriety. 'I can only tell you what I told that nice policeman.'

Jamie frowned. That rather shattered her hopes of prising more than the inspector had managed to get from the elderly woman.

'Come in, won't you?' The woman led Jamie into a small, cluttered living room, the small dog padding silently behind them. 'Now, can I get you a cup of tea?'

Deciding that the informality of drinking a cup of tea together might help Mrs Pascoe recall more than she'd told Inspector Durrant, Jamie agreed.

'I won't be a moment then. Please have a seat.'

* * *

Once they were each seated, cups of tea in their hands, Jamie said, 'I believe you saw Francesca Whittaker that last day?'

'Yes, that's right.'

'Could you tell me what you saw — exactly?'

The woman eyed her with belated suspicion. 'Um, who did you say you were?'

'Jamie Rivers. I'm staying at Moorlands at the moment,' she then added, once more fishing out her passport.

Mrs Pascoe peered at it short-sightedly. 'Are you, indeed? And why are you there?'

'I'm illustrating Alexander Whittaker's latest book.'

'Well, I can see why you'd be concerned.' The old woman again peered at her. 'Are you helping the police, my dear?'

Jamie smiled ambiguously.

'Well, you want to watch out, that's all I can say. Because I'm as sure as I can be that the person I saw with Mrs Whittaker that evening was her husband. They were seen a bit later by someone else, I believe — in her car. She hasn't been seen since.' She puffed out her chest in a gesture of self-importance.

She was revelling in this, Jamie decided. But how reliable was she as a witness? She was wearing glasses, and her sight at the age of what, sixty-five, sixty six, mightn't be perfect, not by any means. She'd already had to peer closely at the passport.

'I wuz taking Rusty for his teatime walk,' Mrs Pascoe went on, 'which wuz the reason I didn't get too close to them.'

Jamie regarded her quizzically.

'They had a dog with them; a large dog. My Rusty's only small, as you can see. A great dog like that would have had him for its tea — if he'd been so inclined.'

Jamie hid a smile. Anyone less likely than Sophie to turn on another dog, she couldn't imagine.

'Anyways, I comes upon them out by Cromer Pool. I'd seen her car parked back at the roadside.'

'How did you know it was Mrs

Whittaker's car?'

'I'd seen it several times in the village. Usually she wuz passing through — to more exciting locations, probably. She never, ever stopped.' She sniffed. 'Local shops wuzn't good enough for madam.'

Jamie got the distinct impression she didn't think too highly of Francesca.

'I don't usually go so far, it being late afternoon, but it's such a pretty walk and the weather wuz so pleasant after all the rain we'd had. Well, I could hear them arguing from where I stood. I might be a bit hard of hearing but I'm not completely deaf.'

'How far away from them were you standing?'

'Oh, now let me see . . . twelve, fifteen yards. I wuzn't surprised. I'd heard they wuzn't getting on too well.' She slanted a glance at Jamie. 'She wuz a bit of a one by all accounts. I'm sure you know what I mean.' And she gave Jamie a meaningful look. 'I'm just surprised he didn't do 'er in before. Making a fool of him like she did. Tales of her doin's was all over the village. What man would stand for that? My Bill wouldn't, I can tell you. He'd have very quickly given me a clip round the ear.'

Jamie choked on a giggle.

'Anyway, they wuz goin' at it hammer and tongs. Didn't seem to notice me.'

'What were they arguing about?'

'Money, my dear; money. I told all this to Inspector Durrant. It sounded as if he wuz urging her to give him some and she wuz refusing. I must admit I wuz surprised by that, him having pots of the stuff, so to speak. But there you are — nobody really knows what goes on between husband and wife. She sounded good and fed up with 'im.' She leaned towards Jamie then. 'I heard him say then, 'Is it Adrian?''

Jamie's head came up. 'Adrian? You're sure about that?'

'Oh yes. Mind you, I've only just remembered that bit. I forgot to tell the policeman.' She smiled brightly. 'Good thing you came, isn't it? I might never have remembered.'

'What else did they say, now that you've remembered this?'

'I didn't hear much more, I'm afraid. I decided it wuz time to go home, so I turned away. I thought I heard him shout, 'You bitch,' and she shouted back, 'Leave me alone. I'm not your banker,' and that wuz all. I left them to it and came home.'

'And the man she was with looked like her husband, Alexander?'

'Yes, he wuz tall, just like Mr Whittaker. Brown hair, broad shoulders — 'course, I could only see the back of him.'

'And what time was this?'

She considered the question carefully before saying, 'Well, I left the house at five thirty, so it would have been about six, six fifteen.'

'And was the light good?'

'Not really; it had clouded over a bit. Quite dark clouds, now I come to think of it. That's why I decided to hurry home. It looked like rain again.'

'So if you only saw the man's back

and the light wasn't particularly good, how can you be sure it was Mr Whittaker?'

'He looked so familiar. As if I knew him. I'm always spotting him round the village. The only one of the family that visits.' She gave another sniff.

'Is there anything else you can remember that you didn't tell the inspector?'

'No, that's it. A couple of days later I heard she'd gone missing and I went to the police.'

Jamie climbed back into her car. It didn't make sense. Why would Xander be pressing his wife for money? And the name of Adrian had been mentioned. Adrian Bryant? Had Francesca been having an affair with him and Xander found out? But would he continue to work with the man who was seeing his wife? It didn't seem likely. It had to be another Adrian. After all, it wasn't an uncommon name.

Nonetheless, she would tell DI Durrant what Mrs Pascoe had said.

* * *

Three days later, Adrian arrived at Moorlands. It was late afternoon, so Jamie presumed he would be spending the night. She had been working flat out and had managed to complete six watercolour paintings and two oils. Hopefully he would approve of them and agree to include them in the book. If not, she'd have to begin all over again.

She had just finished setting out the work on a large table in the studio when Adrian and Xander walked in. They were talking in low voices but she did hear Adrian say, ' . . . had a visit from the police — about Francesca. They asked me if I knew anything about her disappearance. I told them I knew absolutely nothing. Why on earth would they think I did? The inspector — Durrant — said they were contacting everyone who'd known her.' She saw Xander give him a glance, but he made no comment.

Jamie watched them closely but couldn't detect any suggestion of distrust or reserve in their manner towards each other, which would seem to indicate that if there had been something going on between Adrian and her sister, Xander hadn't known about it. Durrant hadn't wasted any time in acting upon what Mrs Pascoe had told her, but as Adrian was here, a free man, Durrant must have believed his denial of knowing anything about his client's wife's disappearance.

Xander had already seen the most recent paintings. Jamie had made a point of waylaying him as he came in the previous evening and had shown them to him. He'd looked very tired, but he had studied them at some length and had given her his approval.

Adrian greeted her now with warmth, his gaze passing over her appreciatively as he strolled across to where she stood. 'This Devon air must suit you. You look positively ravishing.' He placed an arm around her waist and dropped a kiss upon her cheek.

Jamie glanced across at Xander and saw his mouth tightening, his jaw hardening. This was almost instantly replaced by a look of weary cynicism, as if it was exactly what he had expected.

'Jamie,' he spoke curtly, 'show Adrian the paintings.'

'Of course.' Somehow she managed to hide her irritation at his tone, but nevertheless slid free of Adrian's lingering grasp. She wasn't going to let him goad her into rash retaliation and thus jeopardise her position here. She knew what Xander was thinking; she'd have to be pretty stupid not to. He thought she and Adrian had something going between them of a romantic nature, and that was the reason for Adrian offering her the chance to provide the artwork above other male and more experienced artists. Silently, she indicated the work on show.

'Oh, sweetie, these are fabulous. I knew you could do it,' Adrian enthused. 'What do you think, Xander? Exactly what we had in mind, eh?'

'Quite,' was Xander's laconic response to this show of enthusiasm.

Adrian, blissfully impervious to the increasingly charged atmosphere between the other two people, again slid his arm around Jamie. And once more, Jamie found herself the focus of Xander's thinly veiled contempt.

Her first instinct was to pull away from Adrian; her second to rage at Xander for his insulting assumption. Did her ability, her artistic skill, count for nothing? Did he suppose that she could only get work on the basis of her sexuality and looks?

'I especially like this one.' Adrian picked up the small oil painting of the two kingfishers. It was her favourite too, so she was especially gratified at his singling it out. This was the only one Xander hadn't seen. She hadn't finished it until a couple of hours ago; the paint was still wet.

'What do you think, Xander?' she asked. 'I know you asked for it to be done in watercolours, but I thought it would lend itself to the richness of oil paint. If you don't like it, then of course I will do another, in watercolour.'

Xander didn't speak for a moment. He was staring at the painting with its jewel-like colours. If he had taken the trouble to look at Jamie he would have seen the glint in her eye, a defiant glint that totally belied the honeyed sweetness of her tone. But all of a sudden he did look at her, and so caught the challenge in her expression. His narrowed gaze swept over her as she stood before him, one hand on her hip, her head thrown back and her breasts thrust out, her breathing accelerating as she stared provocatively at him.

He said nothing at first, simply letting his gaze slide slowly over every inch of her, before a small smile tilted his mouth and the gold flecks appeared within the depths of his eyes. He said very softly, 'Oh, rest assured, Jamie, I like it. In fact, I think it's gorgeous. I can't find any fault with it at all.'

Jamie was helpless beneath that look.

Her body tingled with desire, with the need to feel his touch upon her. It was as clear as day: he wasn't talking about the painting, he was talking about her. Her subsequent blush was fiery and totally revealing, so she was incensed to hear his deep-throated chuckle as he turned back to a laughing Adrian. So much for her bold pose.

Xander had, with a smouldering glance and a few well-chosen words, effortlessly acquired the upper hand, and it was mortifying.

8

Adrian chuckled, not helping at all in what was fast developing into something of a situation — and an embarrassing situation, at that — for Jamie, at least. She felt naked, exposed, totally vulnerable; her emotions on display for both men to laugh at. He then compounded her sense of mortification by saying, 'And here I've been all this time worrying about the pair of you, cloistered here together. All for nothing, by the looks of it. A blind man could see that you're getting along just fine.'

'Xander,' a syrupy voice called from the hallway below.

'Up here, Rosamund,' Xander called back, still without averting his gaze from Jamie's hotly flushed cheeks.

The wretched man was perfectly well aware of the effect he was having upon her, Jamie decided, and was not bothering to hide his enjoyment of the fact. But more to the point, she would have said he was going out of his way to actually prolong her discomfort. Had he guessed how she was starting to feel about him, after the way she'd responded to their kiss in Francesca's bedroom? And was he now callously playing on those feelings?

She bit her bottom lip and turned away from the amused scrutiny of both men. Were they ganging up on her? It was beginning to look like it. Ignoring them both, she busied herself straightening the paintings that Adrian had lifted up and then so haphazardly put down again.

'Ah, here you are,' Rosamund declared as she walked into the studio. Her eyes moved directly to Adrian, and it was very evident to Jamie that she hadn't met him before. 'Who's this? Won't you introduce me, Xander darling?' she drawled, with a deliberately provocative glance at Adrian. 'Xander darling' obligingly complied. As for Jamie, she still seethed with indignation.

'Adrian,' Xander began, 'meet Rosamund Matthews. Rosamund, meet my publisher, Adrian Bryant.' This was spoken in the driest of tones. 'Rosamund is my nearest neighbour, Adrian,' he went on, the glint in his eye indicating he knew exactly the sort of response he would get from the other man. He slanted a glance at Jamie — watching for her reaction to the inevitable flirtation between Adrian and Rosamund? Well, she was damned if she was going to show anything — which wouldn't be any great effort, because she didn't give a toss about how Adrian responded to the other woman's come-on. However, if her lack of any sort of response disappointed Xander, Adrian more than made up for it.

'Is she, now?' he breathed. 'Lucky you, Xander old man.' His gaze slid appreciatively, almost lustfully, over Rosamund.

Not unexpectedly, Rosamund literally preened beneath the undisguised admiration, smoothing down her tight-fitting dress, thrusting her breasts forward, making sure every attractive inch of her was on display. Even Xander was regarding her with admiration. As a result, Jamie felt drab and uninteresting in her working garb — which she had a very strong suspicion Xander was fully aware of, even though he wasn't looking at her.

She was very careful after that to conceal her jaundiced response to Rosamund's flirting. With a handsome man on either side of her, the other woman was in her element. There were no girlish blushes from her in response to Adrian's bold remarks. She was seduction personified, yet at the same time elegant and poised and utterly self-assured. It was all Jamie could do not to grind her teeth in sheer exasperation.

'I was just about to invite Xander and Jamie out for dinner. Perhaps you'd like to join us?' Adrian murmured in a low tone, his expression such that Jamie wondered whether he had indeed made a move on Francesca at some point. He certainly seemed extremely practised in the art of flattering a woman.

So it wasn't totally surprising when Rosamund purred, 'I'd love to.'

'Good. That okay with you, Xander?' Adrian asked, clearly as an afterthought. 'It will even up the numbers. I always feel a threesome is an awkward number, don't you?'

Xander ignored the deliberate innuendo of this question and merely shrugged his shoulders in assent.

'I'll need to change in that case,' Jamie said, indicating her cropped cotton trousers and shirt.

'Fine. We'll wait for you.' Xander's expression as he looked at her was impartial to the point of rudeness. It obviously didn't matter to him what she wore, not now that he had his lovely neighbour to feast his eyes on. Again, Jamie gritted her teeth.

'Don't bother to change,' Rosamund put in then. 'We all know you're here to work after all, not to socialise.' And with a pointed smile, she turned back to Adrian again.

'Okay,' Jamie ground out, 'I won't, then.' Rosamund was right; she was only here to work.

She felt Adrian's gaze upon her and glanced his way. He winked at her and said, 'We'll wait for you, Jamie, if you really want to change — not that you don't look fine to me.'

Not needing a second bidding, Jamie rushed down the hallway to her room, opened the wardrobe and pulled out the one and only dress she'd brought with her, the one she'd worn on her first night at Moorlands. The blue crepe de Chine. She smiled with satisfaction at her reflection in the mirror. She'd managed, more or less, to equal Rosamund's appearance; maybe she didn't look quite as sophisticated, but she'd have to do. She ran her fingers through her hair. It needed a shampoo but she didn't have time. With a couple of practised movements, she pinned it up on the top of her head. There, that would have to do. Maybe if she didn't move around too much, it would even stay put.

Within moments, she was back in the studio — only to find it deserted. They couldn't have gone without her, surely? She ran down the stairs, and then heard voices coming from the sitting room. Her entry into the room induced a muted but gratifying 'Wow!' from Adrian and a glower of peeved resentment from Rosamund. She manifestly didn't welcome any sort of competition in the attractiveness stakes. Not that she had that much to worry about with regards to Jamie.

But disappointingly, all Xander asked was, 'Can I get you something to drink?' Though his glittering gaze did seem to suggest some other emotion. Could it possibly be appreciation?

'Thank you. I'll have a gin and tonic.'

She belatedly realised that the other three glasses were practically empty; so, not wanting to hold everyone up, she drank hers quickly — with the result that she felt bloated and slightly sick. Her stomach gave a loud and highly embarrassing rumble.

'I should warn you all,' Xander said, 'Jamie has to be fed at regular intervals, so I suggest we adjourn to the restaurant before she fades away before our very eyes.'

Jamie glared at him, acutely aware of Rosamund's frown — once more, she wasn't bothering to conceal her disapproval. As for Adrian, he said nothing; but when he smiled at her, she did manage to grin back. She couldn't really believe, no matter what Mrs Pascoe had thought she'd heard, that he would have made overtures to another man's wife — in particular, the man who must bring his publishing company a considerable amount of renown, not to say money. She must have been mistaken.

* * *

Adrian drove them to a nearby restaurant that, from the friendly manner in which the head waiter greeted Xander, must be one of his favourite places to eat. She wondered then if he brought Rosamund here. In fact, had they been going out together this evening anyway? Rosamund turning up, already dressed for the evening, would seem to suggest that.

They were soon settled at one of the best tables in the room, with their drinks of choice placed before them. Jamie had again opted for a gin and tonic, hoping that this time she'd have the chance to enjoy it.

'So,' Rosamund's voice broke the silence that had descended upon them all, 'do you and Jamie know each other well, Adrian?'

'We-ell, I wouldn't say we know each other well; I only met her a month or so ago. Isn't that right, Jamie? But I do feel we've become friends.' Adrian regarded her with warmth. 'I had no compunction in recommending her to Xander.'

'Yes; I gather it was a case of a quite serious misunderstanding, though. Xander believed her to be a member of his own sex. Isn't that right, Xander?'

'Correct, although I soon realised Jamie had every bit as much talent as any man; more than a lot of them, in fact.'

Jamie looked at him, not bothering to hide her surprise at his championing of her.

But Rosamund refused to be deflected from the way she wanted the conversation to go. She turned back to Adrian. 'You didn't know her before she came to England, then?'

'No, but Jamie's American agent recommended her very highly.'

'It's just that I'd swear we've met before. There's something so familiar about her. Yet, if she's only just arrived in England, and I've never been to Florida, it's clearly not possible. Does she look familiar to you, Xander? Or is it just me? You haven't been over here on holiday at any time, have you?' She was staring at Jamie again.

Jamie began to feel a stirring of unease. Why didn't the wretched woman let it go? It was as if she detected Jamie's sensitivity on the issue and so was determined to pursue it.

She belatedly became aware of Xander's gaze resting on her. Determined not to be cowed by the fear of her deception being uncovered, she swivelled her head and stared back at him; and then somehow she couldn't look away, despite the fact that she could very well be courting disaster if he should recognise anything of his wife in her.

Something momentarily kindled in his eye. Recognition? Whatever it was, Jamie steeled herself for angry recrimination. Should she pre-empt trouble and confess her duplicity? Confess that she was staying in his house for her own ends? As well as his, of course, she swiftly excused herself. She was here, after all, to do a job, as Rosamund had so succinctly pointed out.

However, all he said was, 'No, I don't think I've met her before. Although . . . ' His expression almost at once sharpened, as if he were having second thoughts.

Jamie stiffened. 'Perhaps there is something about the eyes.' He tilted his head to one side, studying her intently. 'But I'm sure if I'd met Jamie before, I wouldn't have forgotten her.' His voice was husky and incredibly sexy all of a sudden.

A silence descended on the four of them as Xander and Jamie continued to stare at each other. She felt a tendril of hair work itself loose and drop over one ear. Xander's gaze went straight to it. Instinctively, Jamie swept it back up, her lips parting as she did so. It was a sensuous gesture and one that Xander didn't miss. Heavy lids descended over gleaming eyes.

It was then that Rosamund seemed to realise what she had provoked with her questions and she hurried to speak once more, her tone now one of petulance as she strived to deflect Xander's attention away from Jamie and back to herself. 'Well, clearly I must be mistaken.' She pouted. 'Maybe it's someone else she reminds me of.'

She was like a child, for all her

pronounced glamour and sophistication, Jamie decided; a child who didn't
want to share her favourite toys — in
this case, Xander and Adrian.

But when nothing more was said
about Jamie's puzzling similarity to
someone else, she began to relax and
the conversation progressed along safer
lines.

*   *   *

Even so, the following morning she was
taken aback to find Xander sitting alone
at the breakfast table, an empty plate
before him, cup of coffee in hand, reading the morning's paper. Adrian, who
had spent the night, must have already
left to return to London. It had become
the norm for Jamie to eat the first meal
of the day alone, Brad being a habitual
late riser, it seemed, and Xander having
already left the house to conduct whatever business of the day he might have.
She didn't mind, as it gave her the opportunity to plan her own day.

But now he glanced up as she walked into the room, and greeted her with a friendly 'Good morning.'

'Good morning,' she replied, hoping she wasn't displaying her surprise at firstly his greeting, and secondly the fact that he was there at all.

He folded the newspaper, laid it by the side of his plate, and seemed about to say something else when Mrs Skinner walked into the room. 'Ms Rivers, there's a phone call for you. A Mr Rob Gilbraith. I've left the phone in the hallway for you. I thought you might like some privacy.'

Jamie wondered why Rob hadn't rung her on her mobile. She groped in her trouser pocket — oh no, she must have left it in her bedroom. Oh, Lord, she'd promised to ring him again and she hadn't. With all that had been happening, she'd completely forgotten about it.

As she'd expected, his tone was verging on angry when she put the phone to her ear. 'Where have you been? I've been ringing and ringing. I tried several times last night, but your phone was switched off. So I rang this number and some woman told me you'd gone out for dinner with Whittaker. Then this morning you don't answer. What the devil's going on?'

'Nothing. Xander . . . '

'Who the hell's Xander?'

'Sorry, I should have said Alexander.'

'Oh, you're on personal nickname terms, are you? How cosy.'

'Don't be silly, Rob. Everyone calls him that. He asked me to.'

'Did he? And what's he calling you? No, don't tell me — Sweetie? Isn't that what the luvvies say?'

'I don't have to explain myself to you or anyone else, Rob. Is that clear?'

'Crystal.'

'Look — I think there's something else I should make clear. I like you, Rob, and I've enjoyed the times we've spent together; but that's all it is — liking. I'm not ready for any sort of commitment. I thought you understood that.'

'Not well enough, obviously,' he sneered. 'What I understand now is that you don't want me troubling you again, not while you've got someone like Whittaker taking you out.'

'Rob, please — it wasn't like that.' But her protest met only with an echoing silence. He'd hung up on her.

Slowly, Jamie replaced the phone on the base, and swung to see Xander standing in the breakfast-room doorway, one shoulder propped on the doorjamb, a cup of coffee in his hand. He was the picture of composure. He also didn't try and hide the fact that he'd been listening to her end of the conversation. But precisely how much of it he'd heard she wasn't sure. Had he heard his own name mentioned and so had come to the door to find out what was going on?

However, his expression remained maddeningly unreadable as he coolly asked, 'Trouble?'

'Nothing I can't handle.'

'Got the push, has he?'

'There was nothing to get the push from.'

'Or has he heard about your closeness with Adrian Bryant?'

'Adrian?' She frowned. 'What's he got to do with this?'

'Well, it's obvious to me at any rate that he greatly admires you, and not just for your artistic talents. So much so, that he rode roughshod over my preference for a male artist to do this job for me.'

All Jamie could think then was that she had read things correctly last evening. He did think that she and Adrian had something going on between them and that was the sole reason for Adrian sending her here.

'Does he know that you're not ready for any sort of commitment yet? That all you want is friendship? Because if he doesn't, then I think you should do the decent thing and tell him before he gets any more romantic ideas about you.'

'There's nothing of that nature between Adrian and me. He sent me here because he thought I could do the job and I was the only artist available on such short notice. And yes, he does like my work.' Jamie couldn't contain her anger any longer. 'And how dare you presume that the only reason for Adrian sending me here is because of some physical attraction between us? I believed you liked my work. If that's not so, then . . . '

'Hey, hey, steady on.' Xander's eyebrows were raised at her outburst. He was clearly surprised at the violence of her response. Even so, there was more than a trace of amusement within his eyes. 'I'm sorry. Okay?' He raised a hand in apology. 'I do like your work. It's good. But really, Jamie . . . ' He gave a snort of laughter, laughter that didn't reach his eyes this time. 'You shouldn't lead the poor chap on if your intentions aren't serious. I'm sure he had enough of that sort of game-playing with my wife.' With that parting shot, he swivelled around and speedily left the room.

But Jamie wasn't about to let things rest there. She ran after him. 'I'm not leading anyone on, Xander — especially not Adrian.'

He swung to face her, his expression a dark one. 'That's not what it looked like last night.'

'Last night?' She frowned, thoroughly confused now. 'I was being polite, friendly, that's all. If you've chosen to misinterpret that . . . ' She shrugged. 'Look, I'm sorry if Francesca . . . '

'We'll leave my wife out of this. I shouldn't have mentioned her. Please forget I said anything. I made a mistake about you and Adrian, clearly. I apologise. Now, I really am very busy.' And, for the second time, he walked away from her.

Well you could have fooled me, Alexander Whittaker, she silently fumed. *You were waiting for me this morning. Why, if you were so damned busy?*

It took a full two hours for the implications of Xander's indiscreet remark to dawn upon Jamie. *I'm sure he had enough*

156

of that sort of game-playing with my wife, he'd blurted out. He'd obviously been referring to what he'd interpreted as Jamie's heartless treatment of Adrian — that she was deliberately leading him on with no intention of allowing it to go any further than flirtation.

His words could only mean one thing: Francesca had been involved in some way with Adrian, seriously or not. Which meant that the name that Mrs Pascoe heard mentioned by whoever had been with Francesca must indeed refer to Adrian Bryant. And Xander knew about the affair.

So — there you had it. The perfect motive for murder. Infidelity.

9

Come Sunday, Jamie decided that she needed a few more sketches and so made preparations to leave the house. As she had seen no one, she presumed the inhabitants of the house were all having a lie-in, even the Skinners. She looked for Sophie, but she was nowhere to be seen either. She hadn't spent the night in Jamie's room, but then she didn't always.

The truth was Jamie was in no mood for solitude. She needed a distraction — any sort of distraction — from disturbing thoughts of the darkly brooding man who was for the moment, her employer, and who just possibly had murdered her sister.

She sighed and called, 'Sophie, where are you? It's walk time.'

There was no response, so there was nothing else for it but to go alone. She opened the front door and stepped outside.

'Jamie.'

As if her thoughts about him had conjured him up, she swung to see Xander standing at the foot of the stairs. He was dressed in jeans and a casual short-sleeved shirt, obviously prepared for a day of relaxation. 'Going out?' he asked.

'Yes.' Her response was brusque and, even to her own ears, strained. She hadn't seen him since their argument a few mornings ago and she hadn't been able to decide whether she was relieved by that or if the hollow sensation in the pit of her stomach meant that she was missing him.

'Would you mind if I come with you?'

The question astonished her. It was the last thing she'd expected to hear. Nonetheless, she managed to say, 'If I find what I'm looking for I'll be spending most of my time sketching. It might prove rather boring for you.'

'That's all right. I'll be interested to see how you work in order to produce those stunning paintings. And, to be honest,' he added with a rueful smile, 'I could do with the relaxation as well as the fresh air. I've had a particularly harrowing week, and . . . ' He hesitated, as if struggling to find the right words. 'I would like to make amends for my foolish misconceptions of the other morning.' This time he managed a conciliatory smile. 'I'm sorry.'

With that, Jamie felt her taut nerves relax as a sensation of euphoric happiness engulfed her. No way had this man murdered his wife. She refused to believe it. 'Apology accepted. And it's fine if you want to come with me.' She looked closely at him then for the first time, and she didn't like what she saw.

He looked drawn, almost haggard. Dark shadows traced lines beneath his eyes, and there were grooves about his mouth that she hadn't noticed before. Strangely, it didn't detract from his good looks. If anything it enhanced them, giving him an attractive, brooding air. He must be having a hard time, she reflected. All the work that needed doing to complete his latest documentary, a book to finish — and on top of all of that his wife had gone missing, presumed dead; and he, in spite of his release by the police, was suspected by all and sundry of her murder, even Jamie herself just a couple of days ago.

'Where are you planning to go?' he asked as he descended the front steps at her side. His height dwarfed her, leaving her feeling delicate and feminine for once instead of dumpy and overweight.

'I'm not sure. Perhaps you could advise me, being a native, so to speak, of the area?'

'Well, if I can, certainly.'

'I need some sketches of a couple of the birds you've listed.' She pulled the folded sheet of paper he'd originally given her from her pocket and scrutinised it. 'The goldcrest and, if I'm very lucky, a green woodpecker.' She glanced up at him hopefully.

He didn't disappoint. 'I think I know just the spot. It's much too far to walk; we'll have to use the Range Rover. I'll get the key.'

* * *

They drove for the most part in silence, other than for when Xander pointed out the various points of interest that they passed. Jamie did slant a glance at him once or twice. He looked exhausted, as if he hadn't slept for nights. She felt a pang of compassion for him. He needed taking care of, she belatedly decided, and then had to suppress a snort of cynicism. Who by? Herself? Fat chance while a woman like Rosamund Matthews was eager to do all she could to console him.

'Here we are,' he said. 'I'll park and we'll walk to the spot I have in mind.'

Trees densely lined both sides of this particular strip of roadway. Xander parked the car on the grassy verge and led her into the cool shade. For a second, after the brilliance of the September sunshine, it seemed as if they were walking into some sort of man-made cavern. Heavily foliaged branches met high overhead, intertwining, and casting a pale green light over everything. He led her to a small, gently sloping clearing that was littered with boulders of all sizes. Luckily, he'd had the foresight to bring a rug from the car, which he spread out on a patch of grass; he then indicated that she sit, after which, he lowered himself down by the side of her. Jamie's breath caught in her throat. He was so close she could smell his aftershave.

'If we sit very still and quiet,' he murmured directly into her ear, 'you might be lucky enough to see what you want. If we have no luck here, the River Dart's not far away. We could try there.'

She shivered at the sensation of his breath feathering the skin of her face. As if he'd sussed her rising emotion, he gave her a smile potent enough to charm even the shyest bird down from the branches. It certainly did it for Jamie. Her head spun as she stared helplessly at him. She wanted to feel his arms around her, wanted him to kiss her, she admitted; ached for it, in fact. Swiftly, she looked away. It was bad enough that she should long for such a thing without letting him detect it into the bargain. To cover her confusion, she busied herself, quietly pulling her sketching materials from her bag.

The realisation, when it struck her, was astounding enough to make her drop her pencils. They made a noisy clatter as they rolled all about her. She stiffened, expecting a reminder to stay quiet, but Xander only laughed and leant over to pick them up. For her part, Jamie couldn't move.

She loved him.

For the first time in her twenty-four years, she'd tumbled head over heels in love, and it had to be with a man who was completely out of her league. So far out of her league, in fact, he may as well be on another planet. And not only that, he'd also been married to her sister. My God, it was practically incestuous.

Without thinking about what she was saying, mainly because her mind was still reeling from her astonishing realisation, she blurted, 'Was that the earring — the emerald and diamond dropped in Francesca's dressing table drawer — that was found at Cromer Pool?'

'Yes.'

Strangely, she didn't glimpse the anger that she had anticipated in the wake of such a blunt question. Emboldened by this, she went on, 'What do you think has happened to her?'

His eyes sharpened and narrowed; she waited, fully expecting a blistering tirade, or, at the very least, a cold rebuke. But all he said was, 'I think she's dead.' His tone was a bleak one, as were his eyes now.

'You do?'

'There's no other explanation.' He

looked away from Jamie's shocked expression, staring instead into the dark depths of the trees. He looked sombre, brooding . . . reflective.

'Couldn't she just have left you? She had her car with her, I believe. It's never been found.'

'I know. I also know she would never have gone off leaving everything that was most important to her behind. All of her clothes, her jewellery; her money, most of all.'

Jamie started to say, 'But didn't she . . . ' then remembered she wasn't supposed to know about the withdrawal of money that her sister had made from the bank the month before she vanished. She concluded with the innocent-sounding, ' . . . take any money with her at all?'

He seemed to hesitate before saying, 'Not as far as I know. And you saw her room. Nothing looked to be missing.'

His eyes bored into her, provoking a flush of guilt on her cheeks as she recalled her presumption in going into Francesca's room and the subsequent discovery of her there by the man now sitting at her side.

'Her designer-label clothes, her shoes: all still there. Every piece of jewellery she owned. They were the things that really mattered to her. She wouldn't have left them all behind.' His tone was one of deep bitterness now. 'No, she hasn't simply left me. I wish I could believe she had. But the truth is, my wife liked the good things in life. There is no way she would she would have left everything for me to get my hands on.' He looked away and stopped speaking, as if aware he was saying too much.

'So you don't think . . . ' Jamie paused. Should she say this? Some things were, after all, best left unsaid. She ploughed on, however, albeit shakily. 'You don't think she's run off with someone else?'

He swivelled his head and regarded her. 'It's all right, I knew about her lovers. Everyone knew about her lovers.' His tone was heavy with self-disgust. 'Except me, for a long time. She couldn't leave other men alone. She had to prove herself desirable, over and over. One man was never enough for my wife. It took me a while to discover what she was doing, but once I did . . . '

'Yes?' Jamie gently prompted.

'Once I did, any feelings I had left for her died. We'd been living separate lives for some time, anyway. I've no illusions left about Francesca. She might have run off with another man, but she would have taken all of her belongings with her. She's dead; she has to be.'

'Do you agree with common opinion, then, that she's been murdered?' She chewed at her bottom lip. Had she gone too far?

His gaze darkened. 'Don't you mean, did I murder her?'

'No, I didn't mean . . . ' But it was as if she hadn't made her murmured protestation.

'The police thought I did. My brother still thinks I did. The police accepted my innocence; my brother didn't. Of course, it would suit Brad to be rid of me. Everything that is mine would eventually go to him: the businesses, various homes, the money. I'd have no choice but to make it all over to him if I faced many years in prison. I wouldn't want it all to be broken up, sold off, have it pass out of the family, and he knows that. Although I couldn't guarantee that that wouldn't happen anyway.' He was looking at her now with a different expression altogether. The bleakness had gone, to be replaced by something that closely resembled desire. Jamie held her breath.

'If she is dead — and I think we can assume she is — I didn't kill her,' he quietly said. 'I want you to believe that.'

Jamie said nothing; words were beyond her at that point. She simply stared back at him.

'We weren't happy, and I might have wished at times to be rid of her, but I would never, never have killed her. I had no reason to. We'd been discussing divorce, anyway. It was just a case of the solicitors hammering out a settlement that suited both of us. There would have been absolutely no need for me to harm her.'

Jamie's breath whispered through her parted lips in a small sigh of unutterable relief. He was telling her the truth; she was as sure as she could be of that. 'The man who was seen with her that last afternoon — you've no idea who that might have been?'

'If I had known his identity, don't you think I would have told the police?'

'Yes, I suppose so.'

Jamie was aware of a deep, deep sadness then. Xander's words sounded so genuine, his belief that his wife was dead so credible, that Jamie's last hope that Francesca might just possibly still be alive was finally extinguished.

* * *

A silence fell upon them both; a silence that was eventually broken by Xander saying, 'Do you know — ' His head tilted to one side as he stared at her. ' — you're not unlike Francesca to look

170

at. You have the same colour hair, the same delicate complexion, and the eyes — they're the same shade of blue. Almost violet. That's probably what Rosamund has picked up on. It could almost be Francesca looking at me, except for . . . '

'Except for what?' Jamie was once more prompting. She knew she could well be inviting discovery, but suddenly didn't care. Maybe it was time for the truth to be told.

'Except there's no hint of deceit in your gaze, or guile. Francesca could never look at anyone without wondering how she could manipulate them for her ends.'

Jamie was mesmerised by the sheer intensity of his gaze. It roamed all over her face, as if he were searching for something, something so elusive as to be virtually unobtainable.

'Jamie,' he murmured throatily. He reached out and touched her cheek. His fingers ran tenderly over the satin-smooth skin, down to her lips, and then round to the back of her neck. His long fingers slid to her nape and lifted the weight of hair that sat there. His eyes went to it, almost wonderingly. He ran his fingers through the silky strands, his expression slumberous. His breathing quickened as he moved closer. There was a sensual look to him now; his lips parted and his breath feathered her skin, sending tendrils of emotion shivering through her.

'You're so beautiful.' He brought his fingers back to the front of her, where they traced the line of her throat, lingering on the pulse that throbbed at the base. He cupped her chin, tilting her head back until she was looking directly at him.

As his lips descended on hers, she stopped breathing. Her mouth parted for him as she pressed herself to him; her movement, if she had but known it, inviting, seductive.

Xander responded immediately. He took his hands from her throat and shoulders, and slid them down to her waist. His arms encircled her totally as he pulled her even closer to him, her soft breasts flattening themselves against the hardness of his chest. She was so close she could feel the tumultuous beating of his heart. His breathing quickened even more as he deepened the kiss, his tongue flicking against hers.

But then, all of a sudden, he released her, pushing her from him, almost brutally. His breathing was still ragged and Jamie couldn't stop her small cry of protest. She reached out for him; she was past caring what he might think of her or her boldness. She simply wanted to be back in his arms. Nothing else mattered. She didn't care if he'd told her the truth or not; she loved him and she would stand by him whatever the future held for them both.

But when he did finally speak, his voice was low and husky — with emotion? she asked herself. But in the next moment, she knew it wasn't.

'Forgive me. I shouldn't have done that.' And then he was purposefully widening the space even further between them, his expression one of resolve, his eyes as cold as ice.

'It's all right,' was all Jamie could say. But it wasn't. She was shivering as if she'd received some sort of traumatic shock. A single question was hammering at her. He had told her how much like his wife she looked. Then he'd kissed her. Was that why? Not because he'd wanted to kiss her, Jamie, but because she so closely resembled Francesca?

Was Xander still in love with his wife, despite all he'd just said?

10

Upon their return to the house some time later, Jamie made her excuses and went straight to her room on the pretext of adding more details to the sketches that she'd eventually managed to complete. In reality, she simply wanted — no, needed — some time to herself, to sort out the bewildering rush of emotion that had engulfed her with Xander's kiss.

She asked herself, over and over, could she really have fallen in love this quickly? And with her sister's husband, to boot? A man who, she was almost one hundred percent sure now, was still in love with his wife, despite what he'd said about their deteriorating relationship.

In the wake of their lovemaking, Xander had taken himself off for a long walk, from which he didn't return until it was time to drive back to Moorlands. She had no idea where he'd been and, as he didn't volunteer the information, she couldn't bring herself to ask. Wherever he'd been, it didn't seem to have done him much good. He still looked tired and strained, his eyes dark pools of exhaustion — and something else, another expression, something she couldn't put a name to.

She did wonder fleetingly whether he'd walked to Cromer Pool, the place where Francesca had been seen arguing with a man who almost everyone believed to be him. They'd passed it on their way, and although it was a fair distance from where they'd ended up, he'd been gone long enough to have accomplished that. Maybe talking about her had resurrected painful memories, and he'd wanted to be alone in one of the last places she'd been seen?

Ignoring the pangs of hurt that that notion induced, she busied herself gathering her things together before they walked back — largely in silence

— to where they'd left the car. He did ask her at one point whether she'd managed to get the sketches she needed.

'I didn't see a goldcrest, but I did get a glimpse of a woodpecker, as well as a couple of others. I'm not sure what they were; I'll have to have a look in one of your books.'

'Okay. Well, if I can help please ask.' And that was the sum total of the words they exchanged.

Eventually, and not having achieved much in the way of work, she realised she couldn't put off the moment of having to face Xander again for the pre-dinner drink that they had each evening, unless he was out. She changed into something more appropriate for dining and reluctantly left the security of her room.

It wasn't until she was standing in the hallway that she heard the sound of voices — Xander's and Brad's; they were coming from the sitting room. She paused, debating whether she should interrupt what sounded like a private conversation judging by their muted tones, when Brad's words reached her with total clarity.

'Oh, come off it,' he said. 'I know full well what's wrong with you, brother dear.'

'You do, do you?' Xander replied, his weary resignation clear to hear.

'Yeah. It's been obvious for days now. Our little artist is far too much like Francesca for comfort — your comfort, at any rate. You've got the hots for her, haven't you?'

'For God's sake, Brad. Must you bring everything down to your rather crude level?'

'Come on, admit it. It's like having Francesca back — but as you always wanted her. You were crazy about her — it was just her independent streak you couldn't stand. The fact she didn't really need you or your money.'

Jamie found herself holding her breath, awaiting Xander's response. Was this when she'd hear the truth? That he had kissed her because of her resemblance to his wife?

'There is a superficial similarity, certainly,' he said in a low voice.

Jamie leant nearer the door, the better to hear him.

'But that's all it is.'

'Really? You were out with her rather a long time today, weren't you?' Brad interrupted. 'What were you doing? And don't try and kid me you were bird-watching all that time because I won't believe you.'

'Believe what you want, Brad. I'm sure you will whatever I say to contradict you.' It sounded as if Xander was having great difficulty hanging on to his temper.

'For heaven's sake, the likeness must have affected you.'

Jamie held her breath, her heartbeat increasing until she felt as if she were suffocating. Was this the moment that her deception was about to be realised?

'They're not that alike. There are many differences.'

'Really? What differences? Their hair is a similar colour, the eyes . . . '

Jamie was paralysed at this point; literally frozen. She had to stop this — right now — before one of them took the conversation to its logical conclusion and began to speculate on whether she and Francesca could possibly be related. It wouldn't be an unreasonable theory; she had asked a lot of questions. Too many for someone who supposedly hadn't known the other woman.

She pushed at the handle of the door, preparing to thrust it open, when Xander's voice stopped her.

'Jamie is completely different to Francesca; she has an innocence that my wife never, in the whole of her life, possessed. She's gentle.' Xander's voice lowered again so that Jamie had to strain to hear. 'Compassionate, I suppose, is the right word.'

'Ha! Has she been showing you some of that compassion, then? A bit of tender loving care? No wonder you were gone so long today. Getting as much of it as you could? You greedy beggar! Was she good? Hot? I bet she was.'

'Brad!' It sounded as if Xander had abandoned any attempt to rein in his anger. Jamie heard a bang inside the room as if one of the two men had flung a piece of furniture out of their way. Xander, probably. 'One more word — just one — and I'll knock it back down your throat. Is that clear?'

Jamie didn't hesitate. She pushed the door open and walked into the room. Just as she had guessed, the two men were standing practically nose to nose, glaring angrily at each other. Xander had hold of his brother by the shoulders. He glanced sideways at Jamie and released Brad, thrusting him away as she hurried across to them. There must have been something in her expression that gave her distress away because Xander immediately strode to her, to cup her elbow with his one hand and ask softly, 'Are you okay?'

'I'm fine.' She forced herself to pull away from him, even though every part of her was longing to throw herself into his arms. She looked at Brad; he, too, was watching her. Could they see the anguish behind the glib assertion that she was all right? For the truth was that Brad's words to his brother had all too accurately confirmed her own doubts and fears.

Consciously or unconsciously, it hadn't been she whom Xander had kissed; it had been his wife.

And the hurt of that almost tore her in two.

*　*　*

A couple of days later, noticing that she was running out of oil paint, especially the cobalt-blue and the titanium-white, Jamie decided to venture into Plymouth and see if she could buy some more.

She was finding the atmosphere of Moorlands increasingly oppressive. Even Sophie seemed to have deserted her, spending most of her time in the kitchen with Mrs Skinner. Maybe she'd sensed Jamie's total absorption in her work and had decided to leave her to it. Anyway, a day spent browsing in the shops could be just what she needed. She felt no guilt about taking the time off, as Adrian's deadline would be met easily; she was well ahead with her work. She hadn't seen anything of Xander — or Brad, come to that. She'd dined alone each evening. Sophie had joined her there a couple of times, sitting at her feet, completely content for a while before disappearing again. For her last walk, possibly, with Dennis, Mrs Skinner's husband?

Opting for comfort rather than glamour, she dressed in a T-shirt and jeans, with a pair of well-worn trainers on her feet.

It didn't take her long to locate a shop that stocked everything that she needed. And with that task accomplished, she could devote herself solely to the enjoyable pastime of window-shopping. She especially wanted to find an antique shop. She was hoping to put together a small collection of Victorian jewellery and wanted a pendant to match a garnet ring that she'd bought not long after arriving in England.

Eventually she came across the sort of shop she loved; not that she'd be able to afford any of the items in the window. It all looked horribly expensive, and the absence of any semblance of a price tag seemed to confirm that. She was casting her eye over the array of objects on show when a pair of particularly fine emerald and diamond earrings attracted her attention.

She stared incredulously.

Francesca's earrings had been of a very distinctive design; identical, in fact, to these. What made her doubt that they could be her sister's, however, was that where there had previously only been one, now there were two; a matching pair.

Jamie went into the shop. Sadly, the young woman who stood behind the counter proved sullen and unforthcoming. 'I have no idea where they've come from. I only work here part-time,' she replied to Jamie's insistent questioning. 'And I wasn't here when they were brought in. I do know that Mr Bottomley more often than not buys at auction sales. That's probably where he got them from.'

'Does he ever buy off people who walk in from the street?'

'Sometimes, if he thinks it's a good buy.'

So Jamie's hopes of discovering who had sold the owner the earrings were dashed. But there was one thing she could find out. 'Um, there's no price on them — at least, not one visible from the street. Would you know how much they're selling for?'

The woman gave a sigh and walked to the window. She lifted out the box in which the earrings lay and, snapping the lid closed, she turned the box upside-down. Jamie glimpsed a small white sticker on the base.

'Twenty-five thousand pounds.' At Jamie's gasp, she went on, 'They are particularly fine stones.'

Jamie walked away from the shop in a daze, her own quest for a pendant forgotten. Twenty-five thousand pounds! Of course, whoever had brought them into the shop wouldn't have got that much — the owner had to make a profit — but she wouldn't mind betting the price offered had been in the region of twelve to fifteen thousand pounds. A lot of money to someone who maybe had debts. But if it had indeed been Xander who'd been seen with his wife that afternoon, why would he need money; need it enough to kill for it? He was wealthy in his own right. His earnings from his documentaries alone must be enormous. Then there were his books.

Of course, she could be wrong, she supposed. Perhaps they weren't Francesca's earrings. Deep down, though, she was sure they were. They were so distinctive that there was a good chance Francesca had had them made especially for her.

In which case, there wouldn't be another pair. They would be unique.

There was one way she could find out for sure if they were her sister's. If the single earring was gone from her dressing-table drawer, then it was practically a certainty they were the ones that had belonged to Francesca. Which led her to another question — if it hadn't been Xander who'd sold the earrings, who was it? It had to be someone who was in possession of the other one, the one that had been torn from Francesca's ear; and, moreover, someone who had access to her dressing-table drawer. Which meant whoever it was must be the murderer. Which, once again, left her with the conviction that her sister was dead.

It all, yet again, pointed to Xander.

★ ★ ★

Jamie didn't waste any time on her return to Moorlands; she went straight upstairs to Francesca's room. The house was silent: no one was around, not even Sophie. Both Xander and Brad must be out, and Mrs Skinner must be having her afternoon rest. Mr Skinner would be working in the garden. Maybe Sophie was with him.

Jamie moved silently along the hallway until she reached Francesca's bedroom door. She glanced over her shoulder, just in case someone should be about. There was no sign of anyone, however, so she went in. Just as quietly as she'd opened the door, she closed it behind her. She wanted no one sneaking up on her this time.

She crept across to the dressing table and with fingers that shook, opened the top drawer. It squeaked loudly. Her heart leapt in her breast. She listened, but could still hear no sign of anyone approaching the room. She lifted the photograph that Xander had thrown into the drawer and looked down at the tray in which the single earring had been lying.

It had gone.

* ★ *

And then, just as if Fate were determined to point the finger of suspicion towards Xander, the next morning Jamie overheard a telephone conversation between him and an unknown person. It rapidly became apparent that Xander needed money, and a lot of money at that.

'Look, I admit I've got a cash flow problem at the moment, but I managed to pay you a substantial amount in July, and you had more only last week.' There was a lengthy silence before Xander spoke again. 'Yes, I am well aware that it still leaves a large amount outstanding, but I can assure you it's a short-term problem.' Xander's lips were close to the mouthpiece of his mobile phone. 'No, I won't do that. I won't subsidise one from the other. They're completely separate. Oh, damn and blast it!' He stabbed his finger onto the phone, cutting off the caller.

He swung round to see Jamie

standing quite still, staring at him, her eyes wide, her skin the colour of milk.

'Oh, hi. The bank,' he grumbled, sliding the phone into his trouser pocket. 'With one hand they give you money, with the other they try to grab it back again.' His grin was rueful and engaging enough to make her heart knock against her ribs. 'Do you have these problems?'

'We-ell, my US bank manager was always understanding. I don't know about the English one yet.'

She knew her words were stilted but she couldn't help it. She saw Xander take note of that and then watched as his warm expression cooled.

'How are things going on the painting front?' he went on to ask.

'Fine, yes, fine. I must get on. Work to do.' She attempted a smile, but failed miserably.

'Are you okay? You seem stressed. Look, if you can't see all the birds and animals I listed, it really doesn't matter.'

'I'm fine,' she repeated. 'Really.' But her reassuring words faltered to a halt. She wasn't fine — far from it, actually — and she sensed that Xander knew that. All of a sudden she had an overpowering urge to confide in him, to tell him she'd seen the earrings, to confide her suspicions, just to hear him laugh and tell her not to be so silly; that of course he hadn't killed Francesca.

But that would be madness. If Xander was indeed the killer — which, at this moment, was looking entirely possible — and it was he who had sold the earrings to raise some of the money he was so clearly in need of, what was to stop him getting rid of her, too, if she told him of her suspicions?

But that didn't make sense. If the murder had been committed purely for financial gain, rather than jealousy of other men, as she was belatedly wondering, he would have achieved nothing. Because without a body it was unlikely murder could be proved, and even whether she was dead or not was in doubt. In which case, he wouldn't have had — nor would have any time soon — access to his wife's fortune. So if he was the killer, it was reasonable to suppose he'd have left her body to be found — wouldn't he? Which seemed once again to contradict the theory that he was the guilty party.

With her thoughts in complete disarray, she swung away from him and began to climb the stairs, desperately trying to ignore the sensation of Xander's gaze searing into the back of her.

11

But then, just as she was trying to come to terms with the possibility that the man she'd fallen in love with had killed his wife, a chance remark by Mrs Skinner set Jamie to wondering whether it was only Xander who needed a large sum of money.

She was in the kitchen helping herself to a mug of coffee to take up to the studio with her when the housekeeper, completely out of the blue, said, 'I'm worried about Mr Xander.'

Jamie turned her head and looked at the older woman. 'Worried? Why?'

'Well . . . ' She hesitated then, as if belatedly aware that she was in danger of being a bit indiscreet. 'I know money's in tight supply at the moment with one of the businesses that his father left him. They've had two previously good customers go bankrupt on them, customers who owe them a lot of money.' She eyed Jamie and gave an embarrassed smile. 'Maybe I shouldn't say anything, but I've got a feeling you might be starting to care about him and I'd like to know what you think.'

Jamie remained silent, neither confirming this nor denying the woman's suspicions, despite her conscience telling her that she should stop the housekeeper from saying anything else. She couldn't help thinking that here was a golden opportunity, maybe her only opportunity, to find out a bit more about Xander's finances, and maybe discover something that would positively clear him of his wife's murder — if indeed she had been murdered.

'Housekeepers can't help overhearing certain conversations, now and again,' she went on to explain. 'I know they've put the business into financial difficulty — only temporarily, but I've a strong suspicion that Brad is putting pressure on him as well, to pay his latest string of debts.'

Jamie frowned at her. 'Brad? Debts? What debts?'

'You don't know, then?'

'Know what?'

'About Brad's gambling.'

'No. Whatever made you think I would?'

Mrs Skinner turned a deep shade of crimson beneath Jamie's frank stare. 'I thought you and Mr Xander were . . . ' She stumbled to a halt. 'My mistake, obviously. It's just that he's seemed a lot happier since you've been here.'

Jamie again said nothing.

As if determined to finish now she'd started, Mrs Skinner went on, 'Brad owes money everywhere. A great deal of money. It's not any secret hereabouts. He bets on horses — well, he bets on just about everything, really. He also goes to a casino in Plymouth. Xander has handed over thousands of pounds over the years, I shouldn't wonder.' She sniffed, making no secret of her contempt for the younger of the brothers. 'And to my certain knowledge, Miss

Francesca bailed him out — more than once, I believe.'

'I see.'

Eventually Jamie managed to make her escape, and went up to the studio. Well, well. Mrs Skinner's words put a whole different slant on things. Both brothers needed money. What did that tell her? Precisely nothing. It merely meant she had another suspect to add to her list. And that took no account of a possible lover of Francesca's who might have harboured some sort of grudge against her. It was starting to appear as if the case was totally unsolvable. So much so, they might never know what had happened to Francesca.

* * *

Jamie arrived in the sitting room that evening to find Brad there, alone and standing in front of the fireplace, a glass of whisky in his hand.

'Jamie. What can I get you to drink? I

don't know what's happened to my brother. He's never here these days. Not that I'm complaining, of course. It means I've got you to myself.' And he smiled meaningfully at her.

'I won't have anything, thank you.' She decided to grab the metaphorical bull by the horns and, foolishly or not, and try to discover exactly what was going on in this house. Finding Brad alone seemed a heaven-sent opportunity. 'I hear you're in a bit of a mess financially. Gambling debts.'

However, things didn't go quite as she'd hoped. For Brad turned from where he was topping up his drink, an expression that was almost a snarl upon his face. Jamie flinched. Maybe this hadn't been such a good idea after all.

'Who's been talking? Xander? Grumbling to anyone who'll listen about his dissolute brother?'

'No, it wasn't Xander. I've heard nothing disparaging about you from him. He's unusually loyal, considering.'

'Considering what?' he demanded

bluntly. Brad was revealing a side of himself that Jamie hadn't guessed existed. A very different side to the one he presented to the world at large — that of a benign playboy.

'Considering the burdens he continually labours under as far as you're concerned. No,' she cut his explosion of wrath short, 'your debts are common knowledge in the village, Brad. People do talk, you know. Especially when they discover I'm living in the same house as you — for the time being, at any rate.'

'Have you been asking questions about me in the village? You're very good at asking questions, aren't you? That's all you've done since you got here, come to think of it. Questions, questions, questions. Well I, for one, am finding it increasingly irritating. And whether I owe money or not is none of your damn business.' He took a huge slug of his whisky.

Fighting by this time to hold on to her courage, she somewhat shakily asked, 'Nonetheless, it's true, isn't it?

You do owe considerable sums of money. Did Francesca ever give you money?'

'What the hell is this?' He stared at her, comprehension dawning upon him.

'I believe she did, and then refused to give you any more.'

He narrowed his eyes at her. 'Why are you so damned interested in Francesca? You have been from the start, haven't you? I suspected there was something not right about you. Is that why you wormed your way in here? You're not just an artist, are you? You're from the police, an undercover agent. A spy, goddamn it.' He banged his glass down onto a nearby table and turned back to face Jamie. His complexion had turned puce.

Jamie took a step backwards. 'No, I'm not police,' she stammered, not realising her instinctive movement had placed her directly beneath Francesca's portrait. She'd always taken such care not to get too near it. Now, in the heat of the moment, she had forgotten her customary caution. She saw Brad's gaze go up the picture, linger there, and then drop back to her. His eyes widened and he breathed, 'My God, of course, I see it all now. The likeness — we all presumed it was merely coincidence. But you're her sister! You're Francesca's sister. That's it, isn't it? That's why you're here, asking your oh-so-innocent-sounding questions. You treacherous, conniving little bitch.'

Jamie started to move very slowly towards the door. What had she been thinking of, confronting him alone?

'You've played us all for fools. You came here specifically to find out where she was. All those bloody questions, every one aimed at catching me off guard. I remember now. She once mentioned she had a sister; hadn't seen her in years. I'd completely forgotten about that. They'd lost touch. It all fits. Does Xander know the truth? My God, how blind we've all been! You could be her, come back to life.'

Jamie began to shake as the significance of those few words struck her. 'So she *is* dead,' she quietly said, still slowly making for the door. 'How do you know that, Brad?'

But Brad ignored her soft question. Instead, he reached out for her and roughly dragged her back into the room. He forced her to stand once more beneath the portrait. He grasped hold of her chin and forced her head up, so that she was looking straight at him.

'Brad,' she gasped, 'you're hurting me.'

Again, he seemed not to hear her. 'The hair, the eyes — they aren't just similar, they're practically identical.' He lifted a hand and grabbed a handful of her hair. He tugged on it. Jamie cried out. He took no notice. 'What have you found out? Eh? With your prying and poking into everything. Huh?' He gave another even harder tug on her hair. Again, Jamie cried out. 'Tell me.' One of his hands was still grasping her by the chin; the other was wound tightly in her hair. She was effectively his prisoner. 'Answer me, damn you,' he commanded, shaking her brutally.

But Jamie could hardly move her mouth, let alone speak. She managed to mumble, 'Yes, I am her sister — and you killed her, didn't you?'

He released her at that, pushing her away. She stumbled backwards, only just saving herself from falling by grasping the back of an armchair. Brad's skin was the colour of putty, his eyes glittering with the light of insanity.

She couldn't stop now though. She had to uncover the truth, however terrible it might be. 'Why? For money? Is that it?'

'Yes — no,' he began to stammer, his fury receding beneath the accusation in Jamie's eyes. 'I didn't mean to kill her, but she laughed at me. Told me she was finished with me. We struggled, she stumbled and fell . . . '

Jamie gave a low sob, pressing her hand to her mouth.

It was her second mistake.

With the evidence of her distress

plain to see, Brad regained his fractured composure. When he spoke, his voice was steady; unmoved. 'She fell into the river. She banged her head. I saw it quite clearly, even though it was almost dark by then. The river was swollen after all the rain we'd had, and there must have been some sort of underwater current. It dragged her away, and before I could do anything, she was gone.'

'Didn't you try to go after her?' Jamie cried. 'Pull her out?'

'No.'

'But what about Sophie? She was there, wasn't she? What was she doing throughout all of this?' Jamie couldn't believe that the loyal dog would have stood by and watched her mistress drowning.

'She ran off along the riverbank, chasing after Francesca's body, I presumed. I left her to it.'

Jamie closed her eyes, as if she could shut out the horror of Brad's revelations by that simple act. She had long suspected that the dog had seen it all. No wonder she hadn't been able to forget Francesca.

Jamie was numb with shock. She stammered haltingly, 'What were you fighting about?'

'She'd promised to help me out with some money. She'd given me some a couple of weeks previously, but it hadn't been enough. Then she laughed when I asked her for more. I was desperate. Xander had refused to give me any. I'd been threatened; my life was in danger, and that bitch laughed. I didn't intend to kill her; I wouldn't have if she'd given me what I asked for. Afterwards, it seemed best to keep quiet about what had happened.'

'And you let the police blame Xander instead?' She heard the contempt in her voice, so Brad must have detected it too. He seemed oblivious to it, however. He had refilled his glass and was sipping from it. 'I don't understand. Did no one see you leave the house together?'

'We didn't leave the house together. I knew she always drove out somewhere and then walked Sophie at that time of the afternoon. I waited up the road a little way. She stopped the car when I flagged her down and then I asked if I could go with her.'

'And she agreed?'

'Yes. Why wouldn't she? It wasn't the first time.'

'So no one saw you together until Mrs Pascoe, at Cromer Pool. It was you with her, presumably?'

'Yes.'

'And she mistook you for Xander?'

'Yeah. Bit of luck that.' He grinned.

Despite her feeling of unutterable contempt for him, Jamie managed to go on talking. She needed to get things absolutely clear in her head. 'But if she fell into the river, what about the earring found at the pool?'

'Diversionary tactics. Clever, eh?'

'That's why when they dragged the pool they found nothing. No body. She wasn't there.'

'I went back and dropped the earring when I heard we'd been seen there. It seemed too good to be true. I kept the other one. I'd managed to pull them off before she fell.'

'Before she fell? That's what made her lose her balance, isn't it? You tearing the earrings off her. You knew they were valuable. You bastard!' She flew at him, her hands outstretched to tear at his face. Instead, she merely knocked the glass from his hand, sending it crashing to the floor, its contents staining the delicate colours of the carpet.

He caught hold of her arms, effortlessly holding her away from him. He smiled coldly, his grip tightening on her. 'Of course, I knew their value. She'd bragged about it often enough. It was me who suggested we drive to the river — to walk and talk a bit more. To try a little more persuasion.'

'But I don't understand — why hasn't her body been recovered? Or the car found? What did you do with the car?'

'I was a bit worried when I heard that

we'd been seen in the car, but I thought they'd assume it was Xander again. It would just strengthen the case against him. I realised later I should have dropped the earring by the river and left the car there too. That way they would have found the car, and searched the river instead of the pool and found her. Xander would still have got the blame. The witness was so positive it had been him with her. He would have been locked up, and all this — ' He swept his arm round, indicating the house and its contents. ' — the businesses, the other properties, it would all have come to me to do with as I wanted.

'The trouble was, after Francesca vanished from sight I panicked. I drove the car to a spot I know on the coast; it has some nice high cliffs. And I simply pushed it over. It smashed to pieces on the rocks below. It was high tide at the time, so I knew the outgoing tide would take most of the wreckage with it — all nice and neat. I walked a few miles to the nearest town and got a taxi back to Plymouth, and then got another taxi back here. It would muddy the waters; no trail to follow, you see, and nobody would be any the wiser.

'As to her body, I've wondered why it hasn't been found. The only explanation I've been able to come up with is that it must be trapped somewhere. There are plenty of places between boulders and under steep banks that a body could get caught in. It was chilly that evening, even though it was August, so she was wearing a coat. I wondered if it could have somehow weighed her down. The riverbank is quite high in places and there are lots of reeds and other plants, some four or five feet tall. A perfect trap for a submerged body. I doubt she'll be found after all this time — if there's anything left to find.'

He frowned. 'The only trouble is, with Xander still free and no body to prove she's dead, I get nothing from it all. Maybe I ought to tip the police off about the river. What do you think? Shall I be an anonymous informer?' He gave a high-pitched laugh. 'They might manage to find whatever still remains of her.'

'You cold-blooded . . . '

'Yes?' Brad sneered.

'That's my sister you're talking about.'

'Yes, so it is.' He looked back up at the portrait, and that was enough for Jamie to pull free from his grasp and make a run for the door. Brad, sadly, was too quick for her. He caught hold of her again and pulled her to a standstill.

'Now, now, where are you going?'

'To phone the police.'

'You know I can't let you do that.'

'Brad, please, I have to. It's for the best.'

'Best? Best for who? Certainly not for me.'

'How do you propose to stop me then?' Which was a really, really stupid thing to say. He only had to hold on to her to do that. Her mind refused to consider the alternative. It was too terrifying. But

Brad wouldn't hurt her, would he?

She stared up into his face and knew, without doubt, that he would. If it would save his skin.

Brad pushed his face close to hers and said, 'I'll deal with you in the same way that I dealt with your sister.'

'You did intend to kill her, didn't you?'

'No, actually, I didn't. Fate decided it that way, and I merely took advantage of it.'

'So why wait till now to sell the earrings? I saw them in a shop window in Plymouth.' She had the crazy notion that if she just kept him talking, someone would come to her rescue. He mustn't be allowed to get away with this.

He frowned. 'How did you know they were Francesca's?'

'I'd seen the single one in her dressing-table drawer.'

'Of course you did. A real Miss Marple, aren't you?' He sneered at her. 'Stupid of the police to hand back the one to Xander. They might have needed it for evidence. I've known where it was for months but I decided it would be dangerous for me to sell them too quickly. They might have been recognised by someone. She wore them a lot. I didn't want anything evenly remotely connecting me to Francesca's disappearance or the earrings to Francesca. I thought a year would be long enough for people to forget about them. So a couple of weeks ago, I took the single one from the drawer, matched it up with its twin, and took them to an antique shop. The shop where you saw them, presumably. I didn't get their full value, of course. The strange thing is, Xander hasn't missed it.' He laughed scornfully. 'This isn't going to work, Jamie.' He had unerringly read her intention.

Undaunted, she carried on questioning him. She needed to know everything. 'If you needed money so badly, why didn't you sell the car instead of destroying it?'

'I would have had to sell it immediately. I couldn't have kept it — too incriminating. And I would have risked the sale being traced back to me once the police began their investigations.'

'How did you get the money you needed?'

'Xander. He usually came through in the end. Didn't want the scandal of his brother being sued for outstanding debts, you see. A matter of family honour.'

'You're insane.'

'No, quite the opposite. I'm perfectly sane. I can see exactly what needs doing and I intend to do it, so no amount of talking can save you.'

'You can't force me to go with you.'

Brad didn't respond to that. Keeping hold of her with one hand, he leant down and picked up the heavy poker from the grate. 'Oh, I think I can. All I have to do is knock you senseless and carry you out of here.'

'Put that down, Brad. You won't be taking her anywhere.'

12

Brad and Jamie swung around as one.

Xander was standing in the doorway. He held a shotgun, and it was aimed straight at Brad.

In his shock, Brad let go of Jamie. She leapt towards Xander.

'Go and phone the police, will you, Jamie?' Xander quietly said. 'Everything's okay; I'm here now.'

Much, much later, after the two uniformed policemen had been and gone, taking Brad with them, Jamie and Xander sat together in the sitting room.

Jamie still shook with the after-effects of the ordeal she'd been through, but she managed to ask, 'How long do you think it will take the police to find her?'

'Well, they won't do anything until tomorrow.'

'But they will find her, won't they?'

'Let's hope so, now we know what

happened and where to start looking. But it is a river, Jamie, and it was over a year ago so she may have been carried further down; much further down. In which case, it could take a while. And maybe . . . ' He paused. ' . . . they'll never find her.' His expression darkened then as he considered the possibility. 'But at least now we know what happened.'

But that was no comfort, not to Jamie. In an effort to distract herself from the disturbing images of her sister, she stared at Xander. 'Why did you have a shotgun with you? You were just coming for dinner.'

'I'd heard most of his confession, fortunately. I was in the hallway. When I realised that he was physically threatening you — well, it was a matter of seconds to get the gun from the cabinet in the dining room. I knew it would be the only thing he'd take any notice of — a definite threat to hurt him. I was just thankful that he panicked and released you. I was afraid he'd use you as a shield.'

'I didn't know there was a gun cabinet in there.' Her voice was reedy with shock, but it seemed imperative all of a sudden to keep talking. She wasn't ready yet for all the questions Xander would be bound to ask.

'It's well concealed.'

'Well, thank heavens you turned up when you did. I had no idea what I was going to do.' The terror of those moments with Brad would stay with her for the rest of her life, she knew. There was another memory that would also stay with her: that of Xander's ashen face, and his utter stillness while they waited for the police to arrive.

'I can't understand why the witness, Mrs Pascoe, was so convinced the man with Francesca was you.' She was gabbling, she knew, but she had to delay the moment of reckoning. The moment when Xander demanded an explanation of her deceit. He would have every right to be furious with her.

Xander considered her question for a second and then said, 'Yes, I've been wondering that, but it's quite simple if you think about it. The light wasn't particularly good that afternoon — it was very overcast as I remember it — and Brad isn't unlike me, especially from the back. She'd have been subconsciously expecting it to be me, ergo she saw me. Don't forget, she'd only seen Brad once or twice; he didn't make a habit of going into the village.'

'No, I know.'

His eyes darkened then as he stared at her. 'Why didn't you tell me you were Francesca's sister?'

The moment she'd been dreading had arrived. She swallowed nervously. 'I almost did, several times. I wanted to tell you, but something always held me back. I was determined to uncover the truth of what had happened to her, so it seemed best if no one knew who I really was.'

'Not even me.' He smiled gently at her. 'But then, you suspected me, didn't you?'

'At times, it did look that way. For

instance, you need money.' Her smile was a tight one; he was looking at her quizzically and with a slightly bemused expression. 'I overheard your conversation with your bank manager. And I knew that Francesca had withdrawn money from her account not long before she disappeared.'

'How the hell did you know that?'

'DI Durrant told me. I went to see him,' she hastily added. 'I told him who I was.'

'Did you, now?' His expression was hooded; his eyelids lowered.

She swallowed again but managed to continue. 'I assumed the police would have questioned you about the money, or at the very least told you about it. When I asked you if Francesca had taken any with her, you said not as far as you knew. That, I admit, did make me wonder for a while; if you were lying about that, what else had you lied about? Did you, in fact, know what had happened to her?'

Xander didn't say anything for a

while. He continued to stare at her, his eyes still dark and fathomless. 'I'd assumed she'd given at least some of that to Brad — it wouldn't have been the first time — but I didn't know whether she'd kept any back to take with her if she really had simply left me. Although I was pretty sure she was dead.'

'You didn't tell the police about her possibly having given some to Brad, though, did you? They assumed she'd gone off with it.'

'I suppose I should have told them, but so much of our private family business had already been exposed to the world that I couldn't face any more. I didn't think it mattered.' He gave a sigh. 'If I'd had any notion that Brad had . . . ' He fell silent then, as he contemplated what his younger brother had done. 'And just to set the record straight, I personally am not in need of money. It's one of the businesses that my father left that's struggling. My own fortune, from my books and the documentaries, is intact. I refuse to subsidise the one from the other, that's all. In my view, that's the sure way to ruin. The business will sink or swim on its own merits.' He considered her then, his expression a serious one. 'If you seriously suspected me of murdering my wife, why did you stay? Weren't you afraid?'

'No. I was never afraid of you, Xander.'

'No, you weren't, were you?' He smiled at her. 'So if your name isn't really Jamie, what is it?'

'It is Jamie. Well — almost. My real name, the name I was christened with, is Jemima. Awful, isn't it? I didn't become Jamie until I was seven or eight.' She grimaced, provoking an amused smile from Xander.

'I don't know, I rather like Jemima.' He tilted his head and regarded her reflectively. 'It's a sweet old-fashioned name for someone who, on occasion, can be quite sweet and old-fashioned herself.'

219

'What?' Jamie cried in horror. 'Me? Old-fashioned?'

'I don't mean that in any derogatory sense. It's a compliment. You have old-fashioned virtues: loyalty, amazing innocence at times, a sense of honour . . . all admirable qualities, in my book.'

Jamie felt herself blushing beneath the warmth of his gaze.

'Just as the way you blush is charming. I like it.' His tone was almost a caress now.

'Jamie decided it was time to change the subject. She'd always hated talking about herself. 'Did Francesca ever talk about me?'

'Hardly ever. She did tell me once she had a sister, and she did mention America too, at one point, but I don't believe she ever mentioned you by name. It was always 'my little sister'. I hate to say this, but Francesca was only really interested in talking about one person: herself. I didn't realise that until it was too late to do anything about it. I'm deeply sorry that she's dead, but having her back alive wouldn't have changed anything between us. We'd both accepted that the marriage was over.' He lapsed into a brooding silence.

Jamie hastened into speech once more. 'Well, I'm not surprised she didn't mention me. We lost touch years ago. When my parents parted, they decided she was old enough at eleven to make her own decision, and she opted to stay with my father. I was only three so I went with my mother. I knew a lot about her because my father was such a prominent businessman internationally. He was mentioned in the papers regularly and, not unnaturally, his daughter was often written about as well. When my mother remarried, my stepfather eventually adopted me and I took his surname — which is why no one here has connected me to Francesca.

'I read of her disappearance at the time, then, with the deaths of my mother and stepfather four months ago, there was nothing to keep me in America, so I decided to come to the UK — to come home — and try to find out what happened to her. Whatever had gone on in the past, Francesca is — was — my sister. She was all I had left, and I so wanted to see her again . . . ' Her voice broke as the tears she'd been so rigorously suppressing finally sprang into her eyes.

'Jamie.' Xander got up and strode purposefully across to her. His expression was a tender one as he took in the sheen of moisture in her gaze. 'Don't cry.' He sat down by the side of her on the settee and took both of her hands in his. 'I know she was your sister and special to you, but, really, she could have tried to get in touch with you and . . . well, she never did, did she? She would only have brought you pain, just as she brought pain to almost everyone she was involved with.'

'Did she bring you pain, Xander?' Jamie looked at him through lashes spiky with unshed tears.

'Yes, at times.' Xander's tone was abrupt and his gaze narrowed as if recalling some of the pain his lovely wife had inflicted upon him throughout their marriage.

'Yet you loved her, maybe even still love her?' Jamie whispered, knowing whatever he said now would very probably bring its own sort of pain to her.

'I don't think I ever loved her — not now that I know what real love feels like.' He stared at Jamie, making no attempt to disguise his emotions. 'I wanted her, I won't deny that, but it wasn't love.'

Very, very carefully, Jamie set down the glass of brandy that'd he'd given her on the table at her side.

'Jamie.' His voice was deep, throbbing. 'You do realise what I'm saying, don't you?'

But Jamie couldn't look at him. Her eyelids lowered, spreading out on her cheeks like an exotic fan. 'I'm not sure.' She was, but she wanted him to speak the words.

He took hold of her by the shoulders,

his grasp a tight one as he pulled her into him. She did look at him then. His eyes gleamed at her.

'I love you, and have from almost the first second you stepped across my threshold.' He stopped then as something struck him. 'No, that's not true. I think I loved you long before then.' He laughed, and despite all that had happened, it was a joyous sound. 'That doesn't make much sense, does it? But I think it was you I was seeing in Francesca when I believed I loved her. As soon as I discovered she wasn't the woman I'd supposed her to be, I knew I'd made the most dreadful mistake. You are what I thought Francesca to be, my darling, and at long last you've come to me. You're everything I've ever wanted. I love you.'

He lowered his head and let his lips rest gently on hers. Jamie responded instinctively; and the second Xander felt her response he deepened the kiss, parting her lips with his own as his arms tightened convulsively about her.

When at long last he lifted his lips from hers, it was to murmur, 'Oh, my love, stay with me; marry me — please. I don't want to be alone any longer.'

'Oh, Xander, you won't have to be. I promise. Because, you see, I love you too.'

The last thing Jamie saw as Xander reclaimed her mouth were those fascinating gold flecks in the depths of his eyes. Finally, she knew what it was they signified.

Love; deep, deep love.

THE END